Magic Mama
Headaches & Heartburn

Katie Fraser

Also by this author

The Realm of the Lilies Series
Through the Fig Tree
Water Off a Dragon's Back

The Shadows of Miss Pring

First published November 2018
This edition October 2020
Copyright © 2018 K E Fraser
Cover Design by Belinda Crawford
(Designedbyboots.com)

Print ISBN 13: 978-0-6480590-3-5

Dedication

For all the Mums who know the struggle.

I'm with you xo

Chapter One

My new Mum anthem – "Can I get a moment?" by Jessica Mauboy

"Mummy!" came the scream.

"Aaargh, Mama," The wailing gradually drew nearer.

I dropped my head back on the couch and rolled my eyes skyward. All I wanted was forty-two minutes to watch an episode of Grand Designs. Was that really too much to ask?

I know it's outdated and I've seen every episode at least three times, but still.

I was barely past the opening music when the screaming started. They couldn't even give me that.

The door banged as the child walked in. Amaya. Screaming her head off.

My fingers itched as she climbed into my lap. *No*, I told myself.

"What's wrong, Sweetheart?" I asked, patting her back.

"Kaylee hit me," she said between sobs.

"Shhh," I said, holding grave fears for my long term hearing if the noise continued, "Where did she hit you?"

It was becoming a common theme. They'd be playing nicely while I was watching them, I'd leave them be and ten seconds later one of them would be screaming.

"On my arm," she wailed.

While I was getting a cold cloth, I shouted for the eldest child. She still hadn't entered the house when Amaya was settled and watching funny cats on YouTube.

I stomped towards the back door, furious about the

interruption to my quiet time.

"Kaylee!" I said, bouncing across the burning concrete to the grass.

She was laying on the trampoline, contained by the safety nets and shaded by the peppercorn tree. And she was ignoring me.

"Hey, Kaylee," I said, again.

"What?" Attitude dripped from the statement.

I thought they weren't meant to get attitude until they were teenagers, not at six and a half, but she had proven me wrong on that assumption many times in the past few months.

"Did you hit your sister?"

No answer.

I sighed and held back the shout that wanted to burst forth and recriminate the child. A deep breath levelled my tone, "Why did you hit your sister?"

"She had her foot in my face."

"Did you ask her to move it?"

"Yes!"

"Did you ask her nicely with your manners or did you shout at her?"

The answer came as further silence.

I rubbed my forehead to ease the headache that was beginning to build.

"Come on, you need to go and sit on the step."

"I don't want to sit on the step," Kaylee started to cry.

My fingers itched again, oh, I so wanted to... but no.

"Well, you shouldn't have hit your sister. You know we don't hit people. Now, you can sit on the step outside, because I don't want to hear that noise in the house."

She climbed off the trampoline, her tears quickly forgotten for a world-class sulk as she stomped to the concrete steps.

I edged around her as I opened the door and accidentally bumped her on the elbow. The wailing started again immediately.

I swore inwardly and bent down to comfort her.

"I'm sorry, I'm sorry," I said aloud, adding an inner

monologue of, "I'm not a bad mother, I'm not a bad mother," for good measure.

"I need a chocolate," she sobbed.

"No, you aren't having a chocolate, but you can get off the step."

"I don't want to get off the step," she wailed.

"Ugh. Fine, stand up so I can get inside without hurting you again."

I knew that I should feel bad about my complete non-response to her pleas for sweetened-creamy-cocoa goodness, but honestly, what are you supposed to do? I didn't want to teach her that chocolate is the cure for all ills; I'd give her an eating disorder before she hit seven.

I returned to the couch to find that Amaya had completely taken my spot and had my phone hostage. Brilliant.

I scoured for the TV remote so that I could resume the playback of my video but the blasted thing was lost again. My fingers tingled.

"Oh stop it," I said to my demanding digits.

I had made a promise to myself. It was much harder to keep in school holidays, especially after spending three days straight with my crotchety children, but I wasn't going to use my gifts to make parenting easier.

"Amaya," I said, "Can I please have my phone for a moment?"

She stared at the screen with glazed eyes, I could almost hear the mark going against me in the mother of the year stakes.

"Amaya, Amaya, AMAYA," my volume increased each time I said her name.

Eventually she snapped out enough to notice my face hovering two inches from hers, "What Mama?"

"I need my phone please..."

"No!" She twisted herself and the phone away.

"No, just for a second, I just need to...."

"No, Mama," She had the sickly sweet voice that only a five year old could get away with.

I had just wheedled my phone out of her grasp and

my finger was millimetres from the play button when there was a call from the back door.

"Mum-my," Kaylee called.

My shoulders dropped as I navigated the phone back to YouTube and handed it back to my youngest. There would not be any "me" time that day.

When my husband, Michael, walked in the door four hours later I was almost jumping out of my skin. The afternoon had gone from one drama to another and I felt a buzz through my body like a 9v battery on your tongue.

I needed a break.

I did what any responsible parent does when they're desperate; I hid in the bathroom with my smart phone.

I managed to navigate through half the day on my Facebook feed when I heard a plaintive cry from the bedroom door.

"Honey," Michael called, "What's for dinner?"

"The kids have already eaten," I bit my lip and prayed he wouldn't open the door to our en-suite bathroom and find me sitting on the toilet with the lid down.

"What's for dinner for us?" he asked.

"Don't worry about me, I'm not very hungry tonight," I tried to quieten the crackling of the packet of lollies I was scoffing down because I was so freaking hungry I couldn't actually function well enough to cook dinner.

I heard a grunt and the bedroom door slammed shut as he left me to my solitude. I heaved a sigh and stashed the lollies back behind my make up in the bottom drawer of the vanity. It had proven to be a very useful place to hide things over the years. He never looked in there.

A battered brown hardback journal peeked out beneath my stash. I stroked it and thought of all it represented; it made my heart ache and my convictions wobble.

The drawer closed with a soft thunk as I turned to leave the room.

"Oh, almost forgot!"

I went back to flush the toilet.

I had never meant to be the sort of hot mess mum who always seems to be slightly behind the eight-ball; always late for school drop off, arriving for pick up just as the bell goes, only packing lunchboxes with prepackaged, overly processed, chronically lacking in fibre, junk foods.

I had thought I would be the sort of mum who volunteered in the school canteen, baked for lunch boxes, sent my kids to school with clean faces, clean teeth and magazine model hair.

In reality, I sometimes discovered it had been a week between brushing their hair, after three sessions in the canteen I had been politely told that my efforts weren't needed and, while the girls weren't ever technically *late* for school, there were times when they walked into their class and then walked straight back out for fitness. You can't win them all.

The problem is, I sometimes feel like I'm not winning any.

Parenting is not what I expected it to be. Although, truthfully, I don't know if anyone really knows what to expect, maybe people who have siblings who are more than a decade younger understand, but that might be the only group.

Today was a carbon copy of most days; trying to get the washing folded and dinner ready and stop the children from killing themselves or each other while facing constant requests to get something or watch something or play something. Sometimes I feel like I'm locked in a front loader washing machine (a bit like that one from that episode of 'Barbie – Life in the Dreamhouse') with a whole bunch of spanners and I have to try and keep running as it spins without getting any teeth knocked out by the barrelling tools.

And all the while I'm fighting this urge to do something that I made a promise not to do before my first child was born.

Chapter Two

Life lesson: Always apply face cream before haemorrhoid cream

The last day of school holidays brought a hastily arranged play date at my house.

I met Trin in mother's group way back when our first babies were only a few weeks old. Kaylee is a few weeks younger than Trin's oldest, Sian, and Amaya is a couple months older that Arlo, so the kids get on perfectly. Especially as they have known each other for their entire lives.

Added bonus; our kids go through the particularly challenging phases at roughly the same time, so we can commiserate with each other. First teeth, temper tantrums, the need to baby proof *everything* when they started toddling; Trin and I went through it all together.

Trin's glass of Sauvignon Blanc had a smooth sheen of condensation when she pulled it down from her lips after taking a swig, "Man, I needed that."

Yes, sometimes, as a mum, day drinking is necessary. This bottle had been popped at 2pm, shortly after the taxi had dropped Trin and her two kids off. She had taxied so her husband could join us for tea, a concession that kept the menfolk happy and allowed us to day drink.

The children were all thoroughly enjoying the novelty of company or a different environment and being blessed little angels who were leaving us completely alone. Well, apart from the odd call to wipe someone's butt or find a water bottle.

We took a lap around the house to try to curb the full effect of the alcohol and made our way back into my living room. The cream carpet was stained with crayon, juice and who knew what else, and scattered with puzzle pieces and dolls.

"Seriously," I said, "I swear this room was clean an hour ago."

"Mate," Trin said, "This room was clean when I got here half an hour ago."

I huffed, "I seriously don't understand how they can make such a mess so quickly. Do you remember the days before kids where you would spend Saturday morning cleaning the house and it would pretty much stay clean for a month."

"Well, yes and no," Trin grimaced, "I think I probably vacuumed fortnightly. Honestly though, I can't remember back that far. I'm pretty sure there were dinosaurs though."

I snorted into my wine glass and pulled it away from my mouth without drinking, "Oh yeah, back in the days where the scariest words we could hear were 'mortgage' or 'health insurance', now it's more like 'root canal' or 'second degree tear'."

Trin started choking on her wine.

I continued on, regardless of her struggle, "I think I'm just sick of the constant list of things that need doing, by the time you make your way to the fourth job on the list the first one needs doing again!"

Trin sighed, finally free of her coughing fit, "I know. Don't you wish you could just wave your hand about and have all of the jobs done sometimes?"

This time I was the one who choked on my wine.

"What?" I sputtered once the wine had made its way out of my sinuses and into my oesophagus where it belonged.

"You know, don't you wish you could just say a magic word and have all the jobs done? The washing folded, the floors mopped, all the toys put away where they belong."

I jumped on board, "Oh and all the jobs on the mother

load! You know, Doctor's appointment to check that funny mole, get eye tests for them both..."

"Oh! And their teeth! Get them to behave just long enough to clean their wretched teeth!"

"Don't even get me started on teeth!" Seeing an opportunity, I extended the conversation, "Here's a question though, if you did have magic, how would you use it? Would you use it to get all the jobs done so you could relax, or would you, I don't know, freeze the kids or something so you could do it all without them interrupting? Because it would be nice to have it all done, but sometimes part of the reward is from having done it yourself."

Trin frowned, a cute little furrow appeared above her eyes, "I don't know. I do enjoy the feeling after cleaning the house, and you're right, part of it is from the exertion and part is also pride, but I don't know if it would be very ethical to freeze your children.

"For one, who knows what it would do to their development. Would their brains continue to grow while their bodies were frozen? Would they gradually end up a few days younger than their peers and fall behind in school if they spent too long that way? Who knows? I daresay there aren't any medical journal articles on the topic."

This is why I love Trin; she takes my crazy and runs with it.

"Hmm," I said, "Those are sound arguments. What if the freezing does them good though? You know how their little brains are always going. Maybe it would do them good to take a break once in a while."

Trin made a little noise of alarm, "But what would it do to their sleep patterns? Can you imagine? Freeze them for two hours in the middle of the day and they would likely be up driving you crazy until midnight!"

I shuddered, "Too true. Any other ways then?"

"What about speeding yourself up? They always show that sort of thing on TV; someone moving so fast that all you can see is a blur. You'd still be doing it yourself, but it would take a tenth of the time."

"Nah. That's exhausting," I hastily tried to swallow my words back but they were already out. Trin's eyes had widened in surprise, "What? It would be, you're still doing all the work and you're moving so fast... It would be like the difference between running and walking. You still get to the same place, but running is faster and requires a whole lot more energy."

She nodded, "You're right, it might be better to just take our lots as they are and stick with cleaning the same room eight times in one day."

"Hey," I winked, "Sometimes you can get away with seven if you let them have half an hour of screen time."

Chapter Three

Something, something, coffee

School holidays quickly became a distant memory when the term started. My Saturday shift every third weekend quickly became my refuge.

You know things are seriously hectic at home when going to work is considered a break.

I settled at the reception desk and checked the voicemail messages, a couple of people wanted to change their appointments, a few new ones. I took them down and started returning calls. Halfway through my list, Amy, the other girl on reception duties that day, placed a coffee in front of me. I tuned out of the call for a moment to thank her silently.

I was breathing in the blissful fumes as the bell over the door rang and the first patient for the day walked in.

"Good morning, Clare, Amy," the little woman said as she crossed the small distance to our desk.

"Hi, Mrs Stratford, how are you keeping in this weather?"

The woman pulled a face, "Right enough, the bones don't like the heat and the muscles slow down, but we're keeping."

"Do you have air conditioning in your house?" Amy asked.

"We've got it in the main room and an in-the-wall one that we had put in a few years back."

I smiled, "Come on, what year was it?"

"Oh, let me think, I reckon it was 1991."

Amy and I laughed.

"And how are Moses and James coping in the heat?" I asked.

Mrs Stratford was always updating us on the antics of her cats.

"Oh, they are just crazy, the foolish things. I keep finding them laying in the hottest of places! The other day, when it was forty degrees out, I found James lying on the hot concrete in the full sun, would you believe it?"

"Cats are crazy. Take a seat, Dr Morgan will be with you in a few minutes."

When the good doctor deigns to arrive at work.

Mrs Stratford had been having weekly check-ups since she'd had a heart valve replacement a couple of months earlier. The appointments had several uses; monitor how well her blood thinners were working, make sure her general health was getting back to where it should be and just generally keep an eye on her. She was in her eighties and we were probably the only social interaction she had each week.

She had the first appointment of the day every Saturday, and every Saturday, Dr Morgan was at least ten minutes late.

The work day flew by and soon enough it was home time.

I made a quick stop by the bathroom before leaving the office.

As I emptied my bladder, I noticed a persistent tingling in my abdomen.

It wasn't the first time I had experienced that particular feeling, as a teenager I had realised it warned of danger. I thought back on the previous times I had felt it.

The first time had been as a teenager. Some guys at school had been mucking around and throwing rocks off a balcony. My friends and I had been walking to our usual spot and noticed the projectiles coming over the side. We were kind of laughing it off, but this feeling in my stomach just built, I felt hot and stuck in my own body all of a sudden. One of my friends moved to step out from our shelter under the balcony when the feeling intensified. I stopped her from moving. Moments later a rock fell from directly above us. One of the boys had moved our way with his pile of solidified minerals. If I hadn't stopped her, she would have been struck.

The other occasions had been similar. Right up until I had Amaya; that was when I realised how similar the feeling was to uterine contractions in childbirth.

Without the additional discomfort of crowning.

I would almost prefer two hours of transitioning over the persistent, pointless tingle behind my layer of abdominal cushioning.

I gave myself a pep talk to get off the toilet and go home to my children - it wasn't short -, leaned my hands on my knees and groaned my way upright.

I can do this, once I get home, it's only, I checked my watch, *four hours til bedtime. Sob.*

I pulled my phone out to find the inevitable text message from Michael.

"What's for dinner?" He asked.

I dropped my head back and gazed at the ceiling for guidance. If I had still been on the toilet I would have been at risk of a concussion from hitting my head on the cistern.

As it was I cricked my neck.

"I'll grab something before I leave work," I texted back to him.

Like I always do, I wished I had the guts to send that one, but I couldn't be that nasty. He was only so inept because I coddled him too much.

I couldn't expect him to know how to pick up the slack if I never left him any.

I checked where my skirt was sitting before I walked out of the staff bathroom. I'd once walked through the entire shopping centre which housed our small medical practice with my skirt tucked into my underwear. That was before I'd had kids, profits for the year would be down by at least thirty per cent across the centre if I did it now.

I wished my colleagues a good weekend as I left the practice and made my way to the supermarket.

The tingling in my stomach had me worrying about what trouble could be coming. I worried that it might signal something terrible happening to my children. I tried to dismiss that thought; they were at home, safe, with their father. The worry lingered.

I walked straight for the fridge aisle and picked up some ravioli and garlic bread. These staples were one of the only meals the kids would reliably eat. Others included frozen pizza and baked beans on toast. Least favourites included anything that I spent more than twenty minutes preparing.

The wretched tingling had me crazy enough to actually *want* to go home to my screaming children. I rushed through the checkout and left the centre.

The heat hit me like a woollen blanket strung across a door frame. I stifled the instinct to retreat to the air conditioned comfort of the supermarket, but ploughed on. I reminded myself home would be cool too.

A toddler's shout roused me enough to draw my sunglasses over my eyes and at least shield *them* from the harsh environment. I turned toward the wailing and spied a child in a trolley. He was sitting next to a baby seat in a trolley that had a two seater set up. The car boot was closed and the trolley was empty. I could see a woman, bottom in the air as she bent to put the baby in the car. The toddler ramped his tantrum up another notch; he was probably as desperate to be out of the wretched heat as I was.

He started flailing his feet and managed to kick the boot of the car and start the trolley on a slow roll away from safety. I scanned the carpark, looking to where the trolley would roll. The roadway was clear, but there was a t-junction in the carpark ahead of him and a car was turning.

The driver was paying no attention to the incoming trolley and turned. He was moments away from impact.

My heart jumped to my throat, the pain in my

stomach intensified, I dropped my groceries and started to run.

There was no way I would be able to reach the trolley before the oncoming car, and the child's mother was oblivious to his plight as she tried to strap her other child into the blisteringly hot vehicle.

As always in these situations, instinct kicked in.

I stopped time.

Chapter Four

Kid swearing – the means by which a general word can take on the psychological benefits of actual swearing.

Example – 'Haemorrhoids'. This word earns its place in this list for four reasons; they can hurt, they can irritate you, they sometimes make it impossible to sit down and, like children, you get them from childbirth.

"Ah Shopkins," I kid swore.

That particular toy had earned its way in my kid swear vocabulary when I stepped on one. The little miniature had been a birthday cake, complete with candle. I'd rate it an 8/10 on the 'stepping on a lego' scale.

I looked around, *anyone still aware?* I was out of practice with my powers I had to think about the practicalities of what I had just done.

"Ok," I talked myself through it, "So, time freeze fields are only localised, I need to work out how far the bubble goes."

A moment before, a slight breeze had brushed past my cheeks. I checked the trees. The leaves on the ones in the carpark nearest me were still and silent, but I could hear whispering from the gums on the furthest edge. I turned forty five degrees and gauged the distance to the nearest trees with waving branches. It was about equal so I'd formed a fairly even circular bubble of time stop.

My moment of self-congratulations was brought to a quick halt when a cockatoo screeched its way over my head. The sound in my otherwise silent hemisphere jolted me to the next step in a time freeze.

"Work quickly, anyone outside the bubble can roam in and the time freeze will not affect them."

If I didn't get on with it a car would come from the opposite direction and hit the trolley and child anyway.

Speaking of which.

I hastened to the trolley to find the third lesson in effect before me.

"Children are less susceptible to any kind of magic," I locked eyes with the toddler, "Hello, young man."

He blinked at me, bemused by the approach of a stranger.

I tried to push the trolley and grunted, *right, it's frozen.*

I thought hard and flexed my fingers around the grip of the trolley. The wheels unfroze but everyone else around us remained motionless.

"Now," I said to the boy as I pushed the trolley back to his mother's car, "That was a bit of a naughty thing you did there, wasn't it?"

He blinked owlishly.

"A couple of naughty things, actually. First, you kicked Mummy's car. You shouldn't kick things; they might break, except balls I guess. Second, you pushed yourself right into the middle of the road, which was very dangerous. You see that car right there?" I gestured behind me, "if I hadn't been here, that car may have knocked your trolley right over and you could have been hurt. Do you understand that?"

He gave me a short nod.

I pulled the trolley up back next to the car, propping it against the tow bar so it wouldn't roll off again after I unpaused the scene.

"Now, what is your name?" I asked.

"Max, and my baby is Evie."

"Okay, Max, can you please remember not to kick out at your car again like that? There might not be anyone around to catch you next time."

"Okay."

16

He didn't seem at all concerned that his mother had stopped halfway through strapping his sister into the car. I'd found that children were like that, they weren't used to the laws of the universe and what constituted 'normal', so he didn't know that what I had done to save him was completely abnormal.

I walked wearily back to where I had dropped my bags between two parked cars. I tried to remember how I'd been holding them.

"Like this, I think," I slung my handbag over my right shoulder and carried the shopping in my left.

I took a deep breath, thought hard –

Knock, knock, knock.

The sound jolted me.

Knock, knock, knock.

I slowly turned toward the sound. Standing at the door to the shopping centre, which wouldn't open, was a man.

"Ah, haemorrhoids."

He pointed at the door, a couple of frozen people either side of him, and me. He shrugged and held his hands palm up in the universal signal for 'WTF'?

Max chose that moment to start shouting again. I thought I had scared him badly enough that he wouldn't start acting up again. At least he was proving that my kids aren't the only brats in the neighbourhood.

I unfroze my bubble and the people, vehicles and sliding doors came smoothly back to life. No heart beats missed, technically.

"Hey," A voice called out behind me. "Did you see what happened with the doors then?"

I turned to see the man who had been knocking a moment earlier.

"Yeah, it looked like the door was playing up. I think some technicians looked at them a few weeks ago."

"No. I mean, yes, about the door, but it wasn't just that, all the people and the cars too. They weren't moving either."

His words were all scrambled and I could see

confusion and fear in his eyes.

Could I convince this guy he'd just had a momentary break from reality?

"No, everything else seemed fine to me," I rolled my bottom lip out and shook my head, "It's been pretty hot, have you been drinking enough water? You might be at risk of heatstroke. You should go back in the air conditioning and get yourself a bottle of water."

"Yeah, maybe I should," the poor guy rubbed his face.

"Take care of yourself."

I left the guy standing in the middle of the sliding doors as other people made their way out of the shops around him.

I didn't feel safe enough to analyse what went wrong until I was in the car.

I thought back to the first moments of the bubble. *The perimeter.*

The perimeter of the circle was large enough to take in most of the carpark and most of the shops, but there must have been a few shops that weren't quite covered.

He must have been in a back office or come in through the other doors, which are always propped open.

The extent of the bubble - a rookie mistake.

I was out of practice.

Chapter Five

Any time they are silent, that's when you should be afraid.

The house was quiet when I got home.

A crawling feeling crept from the back of my neck and down my shoulders.

"Hello? Honey?"

I'd passed his car in the driveway and it was too hot for them to have walked to the park. The crawling turned to prickling and my newly awakened magic clamoured for my attention.

Oh stop it, I put my keys down on the hall table and my bag on the shelf underneath.

I heard the dull sound of the TV playing cartoons, but not at the excessive volume the children usually required. I walked past the office and stopped when I saw my husband on the computer.

"Michael?"

"Oh, hi, Honey. I didn't hear you come in."

There were many things he didn't hear when he was on his computer.

I crossed the room to give him a quick kiss.

"Where are the kids?" I asked casually.

"Watching telly," he smiled.

My face obviously belied my suspicion that they were doing anything but.

"They are."

"Okay, I'll just go say hello to them then."

He turned back to the computer.

The children were not watching television.

Muffled whispers and giggles through their bedroom door raised my hairs of suspicion again.

I don't think I want to know.

I knocked on their door.

Flurried movement met my knock.

Kaylee opened the door just enough to poke her head out. The type of grin every parent knows means trouble graced her face.

"Yes?"

"Hi. I'm home from work, can I have a cuddle?"

"In just a minute. We're tidying our bedroom," the level of aplomb could only be achieved by a six year old.

She slammed the door in my face.

I considered going in to see what they were doing, but decided to delay the pain as long as I could.

I ventured into the kitchen instead. Considering Michael had been home with the kids all day, it was in pretty good condition. Although that shouldn't have been surprising considering he was usually the one who did the dishes.

I filled the kettle and put it on to boil. The pots cascaded out of the cupboard with a clatter when I pulled out the stockpot for the ravioli. I opened the fridge and eyed the wine bottle, but the ghost of hangovers past still echoed in my head.

I decided on tea instead, but when I moved to grab the milk, the space was empty.

"Honey?" I called. I walked back to his study, "Did you use all the milk today?"

"Yeah," he said.

"And you didn't think to tell me?"

"Nah, I thought I'd go get some later," he still hadn't taken his eyes off the computer screen.

The tingling in my fingers built with my frustration.

"I work next to a supermarket."

"Yeah?"

"And I bought some stuff for dinner tonight."

"Yeah."

"I was literally in the section with the milk, if you'd told me we needed it when I was on the phone, I would have bought another carton."

"It's alright," he turned to me and smiled, "I'll just go get some later, its fine."

No, it's not fine, now I can't have a cup of tea. On the upside, I think I could stomach wine now.

He crossed the room and gave me a tender kiss on the lips.

"How were the kids today?" I changed the subject.

"They were fine. We went for a walk before it got too hot, they played Lego, I took their bikes to the servo and filled them with fuel."

It took me a moment to register the last.

"You filled their bikes with fuel?"

"Yeah," his face showed no sign of humour, "Their bikes run on a very specialised fuel mix. It requires a complex ratio of water, sugar and a lactose rich substance compressed into a cone shape."

"You got ice creams then?"

"Yes. And I checked their tyre pressures."

"Well done."

The whistling of the kettle broke the silence of the rest of the house. He dealt my bottom a tap as I twirled out of his arms to see to dinner.

"Can you go check on the girls while I put the pasta on?"

"Sure, just let me finish off something in my game."

I rolled my eyes as I walked away.

I'll see to the girls in a minute then.

I set the pasta and sauce to cook and put the grated cheese on the table before giving in to the inevitable and checking on the girls.

My knock on the bedroom door was met by another flurry of activity, stage whispers and a thump.

"We're ready!" Kaylee announced as she opened the door with a flourish.

"We turned our room into a hairdresser!" Amaya announced.

The armchair from the corner had been dragged into the middle of the room, next to it was a bedside table – a quick glance told me it was Amaya's, her nightlight and a stack of books were spread on the floor. On the bedside table was an array of hair clips, brushes and ties, along with the bottle of hair detangling spray.

"Would you like to be our first customer?" asked Kaylee.

I couldn't help myself when I found them playing nicely, it warmed my heart. I love the way they love each other.

"Sure, I'd love to be your first customer."

Amaya grabbed my hand and tugged me to the chair.

"You sit here," she said.

She ran over and grabbed the flat sheet from her bed, which she then wrapped around my shoulders.

"Excellent," said Kaylee, "We're all ready."

She stood on the step that was normally by their wardrobe and carefully pulled my hair out from behind my back. I felt some tugging as she spread out my shoulder length, chocolate brown locks out and started to brush.

A sharp pull had me biting back one of my mock-expletives. No wonder they always complained so much, brushing did hurt more when someone else did it.

"We've just got a few tangles here. Pass the spray please."

Amaya jumped from the edge of the bed and handed the spray bottle to Kaylee.

Michael poked his head around the corner.

"Oh," he said, "I thought I was coming to check."

"Well, you were too slow." I said, "So you miss out on getting your hair brushed."

He was genuinely saddened, he loved the feeling of the spikes against his scalp.

"Hey, can you please check on dinner?" I asked.

"Yeah, sure, you sit back and relax."

I tried to do just that, closing my eyes as I let the staccato rhythm of the brush being bashed into my scalp soothe me.

It must have worked to some extent as it took a moment too long for Kaylee's next words to sink it.

"Right, that's the brushing all done," the sound of the brush hitting the table punctuated her statement. I felt her lift a section of my hair as she went on to say, "now it's time for the cut."

Chapter Six

Motherhood: where your children have eighteen co-ordinating outfits and you're wearing a bikini top under your clothes because your only two bras are in the wash.

I reacted too late to save my hair.

I turned to see Amaya standing over me, holding a pair of scissors from the kitchen. They weren't small scissors either, the blades were the length of my hand. Her face displayed shock, fear and defiance; a reasonable reaction to cutting your mother's hair.

I leaned over the back of the chair to see the carnage on the floor, wanting to assess the damage before feeling it for myself.

The silence in the room must have gained its own weight and gravitational field; Michael was drawn in.

"Hey guys, dinner is almost..."

His heavy footsteps rounded the corner and stopped just inside the bedroom door.

The hanks of hair on the floor were the length of my pinkie and they weren't wispy; it was a lot of hair.

"How bad is it?" I asked.

"How bad is what?" the innocence in his tone was laid on a bit too thick.

"My hair."

"Hmm? What about your hair?"

My pulse was racing and my finger tingles were so strong I could practically feel electricity dancing from tip to tip.

"Kaylee just cut my hair," I ground out.

24

The child in question had the decency to look down at her toes. Amaya tried the deer in headlights statue position.

"Oh, did she? I hadn't noticed."

I longed to turn and send a jolt of... something... into his stomach. *An acute case of crippling diarrhoea?*

"Michael," I infused his name with my mum voice steel. "You know Kaylee just cut my hair. How bad is the damage?"

"Nothing a quick trip to the hairdresser won't fix. My treat. Now girls, go wash your hands for dinner please."

For once, they didn't need to be told twice. They took the lifeline Michael had offered and raced from the room.

I reached a hand to the nape of my neck. The length was still the same on my left and right sides, but at the back it was a whole different party. The top layer of hair had been cut so that a third of it was now five centimetres shorter than the rest.

I fought the urge to use magic to make it grow back. It was a tough fight. Now that my fists were unfurled, the shocks were indeed jumping across my fingertips. Given that my fingers were touching my scalp, this was causing my hair to stand out as though it had been rubbed with balloons.

"Are you okay?" Michael placed a hand on my lower back.

A strong electric shock jumped to him.

"Ow," he leaped back.

"I'll be fine," my voice cracked, "just.... ummm... just give me a minute."

I felt his hand near the bubble of magic around my body and gently nudged him away with it.

"Okay," his footsteps were much quieter as he walked from the room.

I moved over to the mirror on the dressing table, from the front you couldn't actually see the damage.

When in the Peppa Pig am I going to be able to get to an actual hairdresser to fix this?

I blinked back tears as I compared the golden idea of

a child's hairstyle with the stark reality.

They had played hairdressers with me before, but it usually involved painfully wrapping my hair around empty toilet rolls and a large number of hair clips.

This was the first – and hopefully last – time scissors had been involved.

I allowed myself to utter several choice, legitimate, swear words.

I had no free time for the next month. There was only one option. I picked up a hair tie from the little table and put my hair in a ponytail. I gently pulled the tie down until it was just above the cut lengths, picked up the scissors and chopped the rest of it off.

Except it wasn't that simple. The magic pinging across my fingertips kept sending my hair crazy. Eventually, just to calm it down, I used a spell for sleek hair, which benefitted me twice over. I also didn't anticipate that the ponytail technique would give me a slightly concave cut. I adjusted the tie and had a few goes at tidying it before giving up and just using magic to ensure the style was symmetrical.

Figuring I had pretty much blown my vow for the day, I also used magic to scoop all of the hair off the floor and into the bin by their bedroom door.

I checked the new style out in the mirror before leaving the room. It was a short, concave bob. It didn't look particularly bad, but I didn't like it.

"Mama, I like your hair," Amaya said as I joined them at the table.

Fortunately, Michael had both served dinner and poured a generous glass of Pinot Noir.

I took a long draught before speaking.

"Thank you, Darling. I think it might take mummy some time to get used to it."

Michael appraised my appearance.

"Did you do that yourself?" he asked.

"Well, last time I checked I didn't have a professional hairdresser hidden in the girls' wardrobe."

He dropped his chin and threw me a glance.

"Right. Well, you did a good job. It's kind of fashionable actually."

"Let's not do too much praising while the culprit is within earshot."

Kaylee sat next to me at the dining table, eyes focussed closely on the dinner she was shovelling into her mouth. She was paying the meal much closer attention than was usual; at least I wouldn't have to nag her to eat tonight.

That small comfort wouldn't make up for my abbreviated hairstyle.

My mind drifted to the little brown book in my bathroom cabinet, *I think I used a spell to make my hair grow faster once.*

I shook my head and scooped up another mouthful of pasta, just because I slipped up today didn't mean that I was going to start regularly using my magic again.

"Now, Miss Kaylee," I began, "Do you think there is anything you should say to me?"

"I'm sorry I cut your hair," she mumbled.

"No," Michael said, "You need to look at mummy and speak properly."

She glared at him before she turned back to me.

"I'm sorry I cut your hair Mummy," she locked eyes with me and enunciated clearly.

"I am very disappointed and very sad about my hair," I said. Her lip was starting to wobble, "but it will grow back. It's not the end of the world. Thank you for apologising, please promise me that you won't cut hair again."

The shadow over her eyes disappeared, "I won't."

Michael cleared his throat. I locked eyes with him across the table. His expression asked whether I wanted him to push a punishment.

I shook my head, what was the point? She knew what she had done was wrong. She said she wouldn't do it again. Shouting and berating her would only make me feel bad. I was too tired to muster up the energy to tell her off.

I was bone weary. I didn't even know why, maybe

from using my magic after so long?

I tried to remember the last time I had used it. When it came, the recollection jolted me.

Chapter Seven

I seem to spend my life in a perpetual search for shoes.
Only very rarely are the shoes I am seeking mine.

Three years earlier I had been home alone with the girls. At three and two, Kaylee and Amaya were about six handfuls to take care of.

Michael had gone away for work for three days. After only one day I felt completely inadequate for the marathon effort that was solo parenting.

Of course it hadn't been a typical day either, I had insisted that the girls would enjoy taking him to the airport to see him go. Unfortunately, his flight was early in the morning, so we had to tumble them into the car straight after they had eaten their breakfast.

Earlier in the week, Amaya had decided that she didn't want to wear nappies anymore, so she'd been insisting on knickers, even though she had almost no ability to control or read her bladder.

She did a wee in the car seat on the way to the airport. Naturally, I had spares for her (knickers, pants, waterproof seat pad), but by the time we'd seen him off, had another play on the playground, been to the toilet three times and I'd tried to coax some chips into them, the car smelled faintly of warmed urine.

We drove home with the windows down, which the children railed at; it was how I usually punished them when they were throwing tantrums in the car.

Amaya napped in the car and woke when we got home. She refused to go back to sleep at midday and was almost inconsolable when bath time rolled around at four thirty.

In response to Amaya's piercing objections to bath time – yes, her voice had been shrill even then, and especially in the bathroom echo chamber – Kaylee tried to drown her sister.

Fortunately, we all survived bath time and I set the kids at the table with their dinner. Amaya strapped securely in her high chair and Kaylee on a tall toddler chair. Their food, cutlery and cups of water were in front of them.

I'd like to say that I was feeding them a home-cooked organic lamb and vegetable casserole, but that would make me an unreliable narrator.

They were eating tinned dinosaur spaghetti. Kaylee was eating it straight out of the tin (I'd removed the lid with a fancy pants no-sharp-edges can opener, geez, I'm not a monster).

I was exhausted and had already accepted that I would need to change their clothes again before bedtime because children and tomato flavoured sauces don't mix.

I started to warm my own dinner, who said tinned dinosaur pasta was just for kids?

I decided to make some prawn crackers to have as a treat with our dinner. I grabbed my cast iron pan and poured a few inches of oil in the bottom.

"Now, how high does he usually put this to warm up," I muttered to myself, Michael was the one who usually did the frying.

"Mummy, I need to do a poo," Kaylee said.

"Okay, off you go."

"I need you to keep me company."

I rolled my eyes, I had no idea who seeded the idea of keeping them company while they were on the toilet, but it was deeply regrettable.

"I can't just yet, but you go and I'll be along in a minute."

She left the table and skipped away. I watched the oil and chatted to Amaya, who was trying a spaghetti sauce face and hair treatment.

I tested a cracker, but the oil wasn't hot enough and it sat sadly in the dish.

I fished it out just before I heard Kaylee cry out.

"Mummy, can you wipe my bottom?"

I eyed the oil and Amaya and decided they were both safe so I skipped through the house to the toilet.

I found Amaya bent over, bottom facing out the door.

I think you can tell a lot about a child by how they present their bottom to you for wiping. The more considerate ones tend to step straight off the toilet and bend over, so you aren't given a clear view of your task beforehand.

Job done, I washed my hands and headed back to Amaya.

I heard her laugh when I was still a few metres from the kitchen. Her merry exclamation was accompanied by a whooshing sound, I hastened my steps when I heard the out of place noise.

I gained the kitchen doorway and froze.

Amaya was laughing at the flames pouring from the pot of oil and licking at the range hood.

I paused in the doorway to assess the situation. That was nearly my downfall.

Amaya was safe, for now, a few metres away from the open flames. There was nothing else overly flammable nearby, I probably had a minute or so before the cupboard would ignite. We had a fire blanket hung on the cupboard next to the cooktop, I could pull Amaya's high chair away from the table and then deal with the fire.

Kaylee walked in the door behind me.

"Fire, Mummy! I'll put it out," she grabbed her cup of water from the table and tossed it at the flames.

I have never seen her show such accuracy, before or since that day.

The flames immediately billowed out and reached toward her, I saw the red orange beast move toward her in increments, as if I had already slowed down time in my own little pocket of hell.

To this day, I'm still not sure whether the fire actually caught her, or if I just imagined it did.

Magic burst forth in the same wave of instinct and strength seen in mothers lifting cars off their babies. I flung a shield around Kaylee and used telekinesis to push Amaya away from danger.

The shield contained both defensive and healing magic, which is why I still can't answer whether she was hurt or not. If she had been, my magic healed her in an instant; there wouldn't have even been time for her to register the pain.

"Kaylee, get back," I screamed.

She turned toward me, her perfect little face seemed both drained of colour and unnaturally red. Her eyes glistened and her hand still held the cup.

"Baby," I softened my voice, "Come back sweetheart, come away. Go stand with Amaya for me."

She took a tremulous step forward and I thought she would latch on to me, I fought my own need to grab her, squeeze her close and never let go; we weren't safe yet.

"Sweetie, I need to put out the fire."

She nodded and crossed slowly to her sister.

The paint on the cupboards was charred and peeling by the time I turned back to the cooktop.

Shit, I wasn't at the point of avoiding swearwords around them yet. I don't know if I'm going to be able to get close enough to put that out.

I turned to my inner reservoir of powers and flexed muscles that had been dormant for over three years. I formed a bubble on the half of the kitchen that was in flames. It lay flat against the wall and encompassed the entire cooker and bank of cupboards.

I sealed the bubble off from the rest of the room. As the fire used the oxygen, I shrank the bubble around it, smothering the flames until only the cooktop was covered. When the flames were all but out, I put the heavy lid on the saucepan and contained the flames physically. I let the magical barrier drop.

The emotional, physical and magical exertion left me

stunned for a moment, but eventually the squealing of the smoke alarm broke through the fog in my mind.

The first thing I noticed was the black smoke in the air. I turned on the exhaust fan and opened the windows and doors. I flapped a tea towel at the smoke detector to clear the air around it but gave up after a moment and simply scoured the room of soot and smoke with magic.

Mess cleaned, I turned to my children. Amaya seemed happy in her high chair, still smearing herself with dinner.

Kaylee's knuckles were white where she gripped the leg of the high chair.

I walked to her slowly, knelt down before her and held out my arms.

She flung herself at me so hard I nearly fell over.

A sharp knock at the door stopped me from dissolving into tears.

I hoicked Amaya, spaghetti sauce and all, onto my right hip, Kaylee onto my left and walked slowly to the front door.

My neighbour's anxious face met me when I opened the door.

"Are you okay?" she asked, "I thought I heard a smoke alarm."

"We're fine. I just burnt the toast, but thank you for coming to check."

I tried to smile, but it felt weak.

"The kitchen was on fire," Kaylee said.

Amaya clapped her hands, "Fire! Hot!"

My neighbour looked at me in alarm.

I laughed, "You know how kids get carried away."

I saw doubt cross the woman's face, followed by relief, "Yes. Well, as long as you're okay."

"Thank you, we are. But I had better get these two changed for bed."

He eyes moved to my children. She smiled and squeezed Amaya's cheek. It was a move she seemed to regret, as she pulled a tissue from her pocket and wiped her fingers.

"Good night you two, be good for Mummy?"

Amaya obediently blew a kiss and said "Nigh night."

She earned herself a smile and a wave from the lady. I waited until she had stepped off our front porch before I closed our heavy door, turned and slid down it. I held my children close, probably too close for their comfort, and sobbed into their hair.

Remembering that day, my hand shook as I lifted my wine to my mouth.

If I looked very carefully over Michael's shoulder, I could see the small soot mark left on the wall just below the range hood.

That small stain was the only reminder of the disaster that had nearly been.

Chapter Eight

Me: Honey, can you take the kids to the bath?
Him: Sure
Two hours later (when the kids are in bed)
Him: Did you ask me to do something?

"Honey?" my husband called to me across the dining table, "Are you okay?"

I realised I had been staring at my wine glass.

"Yeah, sorry, just tired."

I looked up and realised the kids had left the table, their plates actually empty for once.

"Do you want to go to bed early tonight? I'll put the kids to bed."

Yep, he could put the kids to bed to help me out.

I would get all of the washing collected up for the next day, make the meal plan for the next week, vacuum all the bits of hair from the floor in the girls' room, and clean the kitchen, but sure, taking that one job for me would really lighten the load.

I mentally organised the tasks while Michael ran the bath for the little terrorists.

I started by collecting Kaylee and Amaya's dirty clothes, then vacuuming the floor.

The girls were ready for a cuddle in bed when I put the vacuum away.

"Good night, kiddos," I said.

I sat on the edge of Kaylee's bed and gave her a kiss.

"And good night, Munk Munk."

I kissed the stuffed toy that Kaylee had had since

birth. It had started out as a lavender Monkey. He had a beautifully fluffy coat and embroidered facial features. His coat was now matted and slightly more grey than purple, but Kaylee still took him to bed with her every night.

"Night, night," Kaylee made her voice squeaky to speak for the monkey.

I rubbed her hair and brushed her nose with my own.

"Mama," Amaya called me to her bed.

"Hey, baby," I said, as I perched on the edge of her bed.

There wasn't much room for people in Amaya's bed once she had set up all her unicorns. She had at least fifteen stuffed unicorns, including one the same size as she is. She squished her little body into the plush barricade so I could fit next to her.

"Cuddle," she pleaded.

I leaned over to squeeze her.

"No, Mama, lay down!"

I tried to protest, but the shouts of my body overruled the quiet objections of my mind.

I surrendered and snuggled down in the bed with her.

I was asleep before she was.

I woke to Amaya playing with my hair.

Beams of light snuck in through the thin gaps between the blind and the window frame. It took me a moment to realise I was not in my own bed.

"You slept in my bed," Amaya smiled.

I stretched, "I guess I did. I must have been really tired last night."

"Was it because you had a busy day at work?"

"It must have been."

I snuck my arm beneath her and pulled her in for a big cuddle. I kissed her on the head and told her that I loved her.

"I love you too, Mama."

A quick glance across the room showed Kaylee's empty bed.

Knowing I should get up to make sure Michael was up

with her or that she had eaten something, I snuggled down in Amaya's bed further.

"Mama, you're squishing me," she giggled.

"Okay, should we get out of bed?"

"No."

I laughed, levered her off of me and tickled her until she giggled.

She had the best giggle.

"Stop, stop!" She squealed through her laughter.

I put my head on her tummy and squeezed her.

"Come on, let's go get some breakfast."

Amaya held my hand as we walked to the kitchen.

The air carried the smell of toast, eggs and caffeine as we drew nearer.

"Good morning, Sleeping Beauty," Michael said, "And you, little chicken."

Amaya held her hands out for a cuddle, he picked her up.

Kaylee was sitting at the table.

"Hey baby," I pressed a kiss on the top of her head, "What are you doing?"

"Colouring in a picture that Daddy printed for me."

She held up a picture of a rainbow unicorn.

"Hey, that one was mine," Amaya whined from Michael's arms.

"It's okay, I'm sure Daddy can print another one."

I tried to placate her before war broke out.

Hell hath no fury like a child who gets angry before breakfast.

"Hey, look what I got at the shop the other day," Michael diverted her attention, "Chocolate cereal. Would you like some for breakfast?"

Her little eyes lit up and she nodded.

There was no evidence of Kaylee's breakfast on the table.

"Have you eaten anything, Sweetheart?"

"Mmmhmm, I had a piece of toast and some egg."

"And here is a plate for you, Mummy," Michael handed me a plate loaded with toast, bacon and scrambled eggs.

My stomach grumbled at the sight.

I thanked him and sat down, a moment later he placed a cappuccino in front of my plate.

I assessed my condition as I ate. The use of magic without full practice often leaves echoes –aches, pains or general discomfort - around the body.

I wasn't feeling as exhausted as I had the night before, it's amazing what almost eleven solid hours of sleep will do for you.

There was an ache in my left elbow and it felt like I had dropped something on my right big toe, but other than that it appeared as though I had emerged from my use of magic unscathed.

I thanked my lucky stars.

Chapter Nine

Sometimes the greatest hindrance to perfect parenting is other parents

I relaxed too soon.

After breakfast I was struck by a migraine that had me hiding under my blankets in my darkened bedroom with a cold flannel on my forehead.

"You know you wouldn't suffer like this if you practiced properly."

The voice pierced my bubble of solitude.

I pulled the blanket down, the air was fouling anyway, and spoke.

"That is not helpful."

There was a sniff. It was a sniff of disdain, of disapproval, of dis-something. She could say a lot with a sniff. It had taken over half of my life to realise how much she could express with a sniff.

"I have offered to help you with your practice many times. If you'd let me help then you wouldn't be in this trouble now."

"I'm not in trouble, Mother, I am in horrible pain. I think my brain has grown and is pressing itself against the inside of my skull. Or maybe the bone of my skull is getting thicker."

"You are so dramatic, Clarissa."

I didn't think the situation warranted the use of my full name.

"Mother, in case you didn't get the message, my head hurts. Why are you in my bedroom?"

"I'm not in your bedroom."

It took my muddled head far too long to get her meaning.

I mentally catalogued the photographs in the bedroom.

No. Not that one either. That's the kids on their birthday. Nothing on his side of the bed... aha!

I reached out an arm and gently turned a photo frame face down.

"Clarissa, that was very rude," my mother's voice was muffled.

"So is spying on someone in their bedroom through a completely innocent wedding photo."

"I'm not spying on you."

I snorted, "What are you doing then?"

"Checking up on you. I felt your wards triggered yesterday, it felt like something big, I wanted to see if you were okay. What happened?"

"Runaway trolley in the carpark, there was a kid in it. I stopped him getting run down."

Mum sounded surprised, "A time freeze? How big? Did anyone see?"

"Big bubble, covered carpark, a man noticed, but I got away with it," my voice was starting to slur.

"What about later? There was something smaller too."

I stood the picture frame up so the thumbnail image of my mother peeking out from our wedding photo could see me as I sat up.

My head spun.

"Kids played hairdresser, had to fix it."

Mum made a non-complimentary noise.

"That's fixed?"

I glanced in the mirror and saw the nest standing up around my head.

"Well, I have been in bed for two hours."

"Best stay there for another five."

"Thanks for the vote of confidence."

I heard footsteps coming toward the bedroom and flopped back on the bed. I immediately regretted the jolting movement.

The bedroom door opened and Michael poked his head in.

"Are you okay, honey? I thought I heard you talking."

"I called because I thought I heard you, would you be able to get me a peppermint tea?"

"Of course."

He crossed the room and pressed a kiss to my forehead. The warmth of his breath brought a moment of peace from the pain.

I smiled softly.

"The kids behaving?" I asked.

"Glued to the TV, I'll take them to the playground after I make your cuppa."

I thanked him and burrowed back into my cocoon. When the migraine struck he had bundled me off to the bedroom and kept the kids at the other end of the house. He was the one who closed the blinds and tucked me in.

He was good to me.

"You'd be better off with some rutilated quartz and some fuchsite."

"Some what?" I looked sharply at the picture frame.

"You know what I said, and you would have some if you were practicing properly, but if you aren't going to listen, I'll just leave you to wallow in peace."

I breathed out and released a vast quantity of the tension in my shoulders.

She was right, I would have everything I needed to relieve my pain if I practiced properly, but if I practiced properly I wouldn't be in pain anyway.

She was also half the reason I didn't practice. The other half was my children.

Mum had always practiced witchcraft to the full extent of the lore. It had led to a very unconventional childhood and traumatic tween years as the other kids started to tease me about my weird 'hippy' mum.

By the time I was a teenager, I was competent enough at magic myself that I ensured any bullies got a taste of their own medicine – humiliation.

My favourite retaliation was to a girl in my class. She'd been spreading rumours that I had the plague because I shared my bed with rats. Absolutely ludicrous, of course, my mother had pet rats, but they didn't sleep with us. Retrospectively, the plague touch was quite inventive. It took a couple days for us to share a class after I caught wind of the rumour. We were in English together and she was taking notes. A small twitch of the finger and her pen exploded, covering her face in blue ink.

It took her days to get it all off her face.

I know because her makeup kept mysteriously fading at lunch time every day for the next fortnight.

Of course, I now know that magic shouldn't be used for revenge. I knew it then too, I just thought I could get away with it.

Two weeks later, after I'd finished the daily skin checks on the bully, Mum called me on it.

She had known since the first, but I think she wanted to see how far I would take it, whether I had any limits of my own.

My punishment had been polishing her vast crystal collection and wearing a serpentine bracelet for a month to manage my hormones.

My unconventional, and subsequently traumatising, formative years led to me rejecting my magical abilities to give my children a normal childhood.

I woke and rolled over to look at the clock.

6:00PM.

I had slept for roughly four hours.

I reached under my pillow for my phone and my fingers brushed on two smooth, cold, roundish objects. When I pulled my hand out, two crystals rested in my hand.

"Rutilated Quartz and Fuchsite," I said to the empty room.

Mother had been kind and given me crystals to fight my magical whiplash. They had worked too, the vice had released its grip on my skull and my energy levels were restored. I would have to charge up some crystals of my own.

Wait, what am I thinking? I'm not planning to practice, am I?

I put the strange thoughts down to my exertions and magically assisted recovery; I wasn't going to let one experience break a vow I'd held more or less unwaveringly for seven years.

The sound of clanking pots and running water echoed from the kitchen. It sounded like he had it all under control, so I picked up my phone to trawl Facebook.

There wasn't much of note; I scrolled past some craft videos, dished out some 'likes' to pictures of friend's kids, laughed at someone's bus ride rant.

I came across a picture from the local police service that had been shared by half a dozen friends, a young face smiled out of the phone at me.

"Police are seeking the assistance of the public to help locate missing young woman, Samantha Rattimann," the post proclaimed, "Samantha Rattimann, 15, was last seen at her home on Friday. Police and her family are concerned for her welfare due to her age."

The post further instructed anyone with information to contact the local police with information.

My stomach clenched and unclenched with concern for the teenager and fear that one day the faces of my own children might feature in such a post.

What would we do? How would such a scenario come about? How can I stop that from happening?

Fearful scenarios raced through my head of my children, older and wilful, running away from home because of a clash of opinions, or suffering from depression through the horrid teen years.

These thoughts terrified me.

I worried that I would be unable to protect them, that I would lose them and that I wouldn't be able to prepare them for any troubles they would face in their lives.

I spent twenty minutes in bed, phone forgotten, rolling over different scenarios; what would happen to them if I died, who would look after them if they lost both myself and Michael, how we would cope if we lost one of them.

Finally, realising that this was getting me nowhere, I rose from the bed.

Chapter Ten

The worst worries are the unrealised ones.

Michael took one look at my pale face and immediately crossed the kitchen.

"Sheesh, Clare, you look awful! Why did you get out of bed if you still have the migraine?"

"My head's fine, it's not that."

He ushered me to a chair. I gagged when the smell of fried rice assaulted my nose, my stomach was roiling.

"Whoa, what's wrong?" his complexion paled then, "You aren't pregnant again are you?"

The question snapped me out of my shock, "No! How could I be? You've had a vasectomy."

The sudden jolt upright caused pain to spike into my eye sockets, I cradled my head in my hands.

He put his hands on his shoulders and brought his face level with mine. His voice was gentle when he spoke again.

"Honey, what's wrong?"

Before I could string together the words to answer him I was struck cold by another realisation. The house was silent.

I managed to hold my voice steady as ice ran down my spine.

"Honey, where are the kids?"

"Tell me what's wrong with you first."

A sudden montage of horrible thoughts inspired by my recent freak out assaulted me- the kids taken, wandered away, murdered. Despite the cold heaviness of my limbs, my fingers started to burn.

"Where are the kids?" steel infused my voice, but tears sprang in my eyes.

He managed to draw away and draw me closer at the same time. He pulled me off the chair and into his embrace.

"It's okay, your Mum came round and collected them, she said you'd told her you had a migraine so she offered to take them for the night. I thought it might be a good chance to have a quiet dinner together and relax a little."

I looked into his eyes and knew he was telling me the truth, but part of me was strangely uncertain.

"Promise?"

"Baby," He pulled me in tight to his chest, "Of course I promise. The girls are fine."

I pressed my face into his t-shirt and sobbed hard for a few minutes. The great press of fear had given way and a relief so vast had filled the void that I found myself crying without even really knowing why.

Eventually I started to feel stupid, as I usually do when I cry. I pulled my hands into my jacket sleeves and wiped my eyes.

I smiled sheepishly up at Michael, "Sorry."

He placed a kiss on my forehead. I traced a crinkle in his brow.

"How about we have some dinner and a glass of wine and talk about what that was?"

I nodded and let him help me to my feet, laughing as he squeezed my tummy and tried to haul me up.

"You'll break your back!"

He sat me back up at the table and presented me with a large glass of red wine. I swirled, sniffed and quaffed.

Naturally, I also choked on it.

Michael whacked me on the back, "You are all kinds of mess tonight!"

I dug in the stretchy pockets of my pyjama pants for my phone and showed Michael the picture of the missing girl.

"Yeah, I saw that, she's from a couple suburbs over

isn't she?"

I nodded, "I just worry, sometimes, you know, that something like that will happen to our kids when they're older. I feel like I always need to be vigilant, I can't take my eyes off them at the playground in case there is some paedo just waiting for an opportunity to hoof off with them. They want to walk by themselves next to the main road and freak out when I make them hold my hand, but I freak out when they won't.

"There just seems to be so much danger in the world and I just want to protect them from it."

Michael moved next to my chair and pulled my head to his chest, rubbing my hair.

"I know, love. You do a great job with the girls. They are safe, I promise. You've just been a little stressed this week, and you're probably all wrung out from your migraine. You'll be alright after a good feed."

We did have a nice, quiet dinner.

Michael even convinced me to have a bath, where I sank blissfully into the bubbles and read a romance novel.

It was nearing midnight when we climbed under the covers and snuggled up for the night.

Infuriatingly, as soon as I climbed into bed I was wide awake, despite having had trouble keeping my eyes open as I read at the couch. I wondered why I was so wakeful.

Of course, the afternoon sleep!

But I had earned that sleep, and I'd woken up six hours earlier, I should still be tired again now.

I sighed, put my phone on the nightstand and rolled over to cuddle into Michael, tucking my body around his.

I tried to get to sleep.

My mind threw up barriers.

Where could that girl have got to? How must her parents be feeling? How would I feel if my kids went missing? What about that poor girl who was bullied and died earlier in the year? How do you stop that happening? How do I make sure that I raise kids who are strong enough to withstand that? How do I make sure my kids don't cause that?

Around and around my mind went, my heart rate started rising and I realised that my breath was coming in bursts, my chest began to hurt. Wasn't I too young to have a heart attack?

I grabbed my fitness tracker from where is sat on the bedside next to my phone, rumpling the sheet and causing Michael to stir and roll over. He threw an arm over my body and pulled me close, taking over the role of big spoon to my little.

I checked my heart rate. 120 bpm. Much too high for a resting heart rate. I barely even crack that chasing Amaya when she's stolen my phone.

I put my fingers to the pulse point on my neck. My heart rate was high, but regular. I was pretty sure that it would be irregular if I was having a heart attack, plus you were meant to get a pain in your left arm. My left arm was uncomfortable, but I had been laying on it.

I took some deep breaths and tried to calm my farm.

A few minutes later my heart rate had settled back down to eighty bpm.

Not wanting to take any more chances, I grabbed my phone and played Sudoku.

Chapter Eleven

Parenting is a constant struggle between being wanted, being needed, being bothered and being left blissfully alone.

I woke up with a headache.

Light was pouring in the window, it felt like a husky had shed its summer coat in my mouth and Michael's snores rumbled in my eardrum. I took immediate action on the one thing I could change. I elbowed my husband in the ribs.

"-at?" he grunted.

"Snoring."

"Mmff, sorry," he rolled over and pressed his bum to mine.

I would have rolled over, but the pounding in my head prohibited movement.

"How much did I drink last night?" I assumed alcohol was to blame for my foul state.

"One," his muffled grumble was barely decipherable.

Bottle?

Only one glass? This headache was on par with some of the most epic hangovers I'd ever suffered, plus the lining of my stomach felt like it had been replaced with sandpaper.

I needed greasy food, caffeine and paracetamol, stat.

I remembered that sleep deprivation is often responsible for more than half of my hangover woes and wondered what time I had actually fallen asleep. The phone was in bed with me, so I must have still been playing on it when I succumbed to slumber.

"Bacon," I moaned.

Michael's response was a great trumpeting sound from beneath the blanket.

"You are so gross."

Bacon, eggs and cheese on toast restored much of my humanity.

Coffee restored most of the rest.

The children came elephanting into the house as I downed the last of my coffee.

Yes, elephanting. If you have ever heard children barrel into a previously quiet house, thundering footsteps on floorboards and jubilant voices echoing in passageways, you'll know what I mean.

"Hey, babies," I said as the girls clambered onto my lap.

I was sitting in an armchair so it took all of three seconds for the warm fuzzies of the cuddle to warp into the beginning of a red haze as the fight started.

"Amaya, get your leg off me," Kaylee whined.

"I was here first," Amaya said.

I moved Amaya's leg away and she immediately twitched it back.

"Sto-op!" Kaylee went from whine to catfight in under twenty seconds.

Why me?

"Alright, you two," I attempted to break up the fight, "Tell me what you did with Grandma this morning."

"We had chocolate for breakfast," Kaylee's whisper was conspiratorial.

"Really?" that explained why they had no patience for each other.

"Chocolate pancakes," Mum said quickly, she must have sensed my ire as she entered the room, "I made chocolate pancakes and they had them with sliced banana on top – three each."

"Awesome, thanks Mum," I shooed the kids off my lap, "Would you like a cuppa?"

"Yes, please."

The kids started kicking up a fuss as soon as I moved toward the kitchen.

"Go see Daddy and let him know you're home, he's out the back. Maybe you can play cafe in the cubby house? It looks nice out."

Amaya took off, but Kaylee eyed me.

"Why do you always say that?"

"What?" I was only half paying attention to her as I topped up the kettle.

"You always say, 'It's a nice day, you should play in your cubby,' Why?"

Nothing came to me but honesty, "Because Mummy and Daddy paid a lot of money for you to have that lovely cubby house and I'd like you to play in it. A lot."

"Okay," she smiled and took off.

I made tea and Mum and I sat down at the solid wood dining table.

"How are you holding up?" Mum asked.

"What do you mean?" I blew on my tea.

She studied me for a few moments. I saw her eyes lose focus slightly and knew she was reading my aura.

"Good grief, Clare! Your aura is a mess, you've got a positive chaos of colours going on there, and I see entirely too much black for my liking. What is wrong?"

I instinctively threw up a shield to protect my aura from further scrying. A lack of practice of magic did not equate to a lack of knowledge.

"Mum, I've asked you not to read my aura," my temper flared up as hot as my tea. I concentrated on calming myself lest my aura shield collapse.

"Great shield," Mum said, "I can barely even spy any leakage." Her eyes shimmered silver as she cast her gaze over me.

She stuck her head under the table, only to bob back up a few seconds later.

"No leakage at all, you even covered your nether regions, there are usually a lot of emanations from there and people simply forget about it."

After thirty two years on the earth, almost ten years of marriage and two kids, her comment still made me blush.

"Mu-um! Honestly, this is why I don't practice! All through my childhood you would just look at my aura and work out what was wrong. When you noticed that all the chocolate had been eaten you would cast a spell for honesty. If money went missing from your purse you would scry the past in a bowl of water. We had no chance for any sort of normal childhood, we were too busy trying not to let other kids know just how crazy things were in our home."

"Talk about crazy, do you remember that time you found my magic book and made that weird golden camel come to life? I got home from work and there were you kids chasing this tinkling thing around the house-"

"Not funny, Mum."

She sobered, "Well, you never would have been so good at hiding your emotions if I hadn't read them from time to time.

"What is bothering you, honey?" A gentleness came into her tone and she reached out and touched my hand.

"Everything... and nothing. It's all just so hard, you know? Get the kids to school, go to work, pick them up, make their lunches, make their dinner, get them clean, make sure their clothes are clean, and once you've done all the jobs, five more have cropped up and you need to start from the top again anyway.

"I just feel like I'm in a constant state of motion, but very little of it is actually of benefit to me."

Mum's eyes took on a shadowy cast.

"I know love, it's hard..."

"Do you though? In your generation women didn't have to work outside the home. Houses cost a fifth of what they do now and were affordable on a single wage. Sometimes I feel like feminism was a bad idea.

"'Let's work outside of the home', they said, 'it'll be great', they said. They started buying houses that could only be afforded by couples with a dual income and all of a sudden you need a wage to cover the mortgage and one to pay the bills and buy the groceries.

"On one hand I love that I have the reason and the motivation and the opportunity to leave the house and have conversations with other adults, but on the other I feel incredibly stuck because I'm meant to work like I don't have kids and parent like I don't have a job.

"It's just..." the words finally falter, "tough."

Mum just looked at me with pity in her eyes, apparently lost for words.

"Well, maybe you wouldn't have to work so much if you worked somewhere you could use your qualifications fully..."

"We've had this conversation too. I've seen the Mums with the high flying careers and some of them seem to have an even worse time of it. They may only spend two or three days at the office, but they have to spend at least twice that working at home to prove that they are worthy of their positions. Or they work full time and battle with the mother guilt.

"I don't know if there is a solution, if it's just our generation who will have to face these troubles. Maybe the kids raised in these households will see what toll is taken on the mothers and society will come to accept us and see the value of us, but right now it's just a bit shit."

I leaned forward and stared into my cup of tea, maybe its golden depths would hold the answers.

"Clare," Mum beseeched.

"No, Mum, it's fine," the weight on my shoulders disagreed with my words, "I'll be fine. I just, I think I just need a little quiet time at the moment."

She reached over and squeezed my hand.

"Come on," she picked up her tea, "Let's go and enjoy these cups out in the sunshine."

We spent a happy half an hour sitting in the sunshine being served cakes and drinks from the kid's cafe.

I drained my tea cup and dodged the crumbs from the chocolate biscuits I'd dunked in there while it was still hot.

"Well, I guess I should get the jobs started, I really

should have got the washing done yesterday and I want to change the bed sheets."

Mum stood first and pressed a hand to my shoulder, "I'll get it, Clare. You stay out here in the sunshine, get your Vitamin D levels up."

"What would you know about my Vitamin D levels?" I half-heartedly sassed.

"That despite being a country of sunshine and summer, around 25% of Australians have Vitamin D deficiency. Now, stay there and relax."

Michael joined me just as I was starting to nod off.

"Did your Mum go home?"

"No, she's helping with the cleaning," I said without thinking.

"What?" he half-rose from his seat.

"Sit down," I said wearily.

He complied, "You know I don't like it when other people clean our house."

"She's not 'other people', she's my Mum. She's literally been cleaning up after me for my whole life."

"Still, if you're too tired to do the housework, I'll do it."

It was a conversation we'd had many times before. He says he doesn't want anyone else to clean our house; I say I don't have time. He says he'll do the housework; I say he doesn't have time either. The house becomes a tip, Mum cleans it up and we have the conversation all over again. It was getting old.

"She likes helping."

He didn't answer but I could feel the impatience rolling off him.

He rose after five minutes, "I'll go see if she needs help."

"No need," Mum breezed out the door and sat in Michael's vacated chair. "I'm finished, but you can make me another cuppa if you like."

He bustled into the house, the door slamming behind him.

He re-emerged with a cup of tea and a plate of biscuits

and cheese a few minutes later.

"The house is spotless," he said, "How did you do that so quickly? I didn't even hear the vacuum, Clare takes half the day and it still doesn't look that good."

My inferiority complex warred with indignation.

"Well, it's always easier when the kids aren't in the way."

And when you use magic, I didn't realise I had projected my thought until Mum turned a benevolent smile on me.

"Yeah, well, some kind of magic, I reckon," Michael said.

I felt myself flush; worried that he must have caught a hint of my thought.

Mum laughed it off, "Yes, using magic for housework. Although, I feel that would be a terrible waste of magic, don't you?"

"It would be easier than scrubbing the stains in the bathroom grout with a toothbrush!" he joined in the liveliness.

"When was the last time you tried to clean the grout in the bathroom?" I growled.

He looked at me, hurt, stricken and a little indignant himself, "Relax, Clare, it was a joke. I guess I'll go get something sorted for lunch."

I dropped my head back on the couch and sighed.

Nothing was going right.

I was chopping vegies for dinner when I heard a tap on glass. I dismissed it as my imagination – Michael had taken the girls to the shops to get garlic bread, not that we really needed it, I just needed them out of the house.

The tapping came again - this time matching the beat of the music I had playing.

I looked to the window over the kitchen sink and saw two galahs sitting the window sill.

I dropped the knife, rubbed my eyes and looked again. The birds were still there.

I took a slow step toward the window, not wanting to

scare the birds, but the closest was not cowed. He tapped on the window with his beak, busting out a new rhythm.

"Alright, hold your horses, I'm coming."

I crossed the kitchen and tossed the sash window up. The screen had been missing for several years, so the birds jumped straight in as soon as it was opened and started chattering at me.

"Whoa, whoa, whoa," I said, "Slow down, can't you hear how the noise echoes in here?"

The cacophony ceased and then started again in bursts as each bird started speaking and then stopped when they realised the other was talking. They dissolved into bickering, battling beaks until I silenced them again.

"Right! Stop it you two! Goodness gracious me," I pointed to the bird on the left, "You first."

"Cheech, cheech," it sang, "Clare! Joy to meet!"

"Took my words!" the other bird said. They started bickering again.

"You two!"

They stopped again and tucked their heads down, puffing up their feathers and stepping away from each other.

I studied the birds closely.

Seeing birds around the house was another thing I was used to as a child.

Birds sense the use of magic and are naturally curious creatures. We were constantly visited by birds ranging in size from honeyeaters to sulpur-crested cockatoos. Once, when we were on holiday in the country, we even had a wedge tailed eagle stop by for a chat.

I looked into the eyes of the nearest parrot and joy bubbled up inside me as I held out my hand.

"Dash?! Eneya?!"

The galahs climbed up my arms and snuggled on my shoulders. They chewed my hair and let me scratch their neck feathers.

Tears pricked my eyes, "Oh, you two! I haven't seen you in I don't even know how long."

"Twelve years," Dash said in my left ear.

"Hush," Eneya said in my right, "Don't answer asks like that. Reminds them, not hatchlings. Is an erotical question."

I snort laughed, "I think you mean 'rhetorical' question, has Mum been trying to teach you human habits again?"

"Constantly," Dash said quietly in my left ear as Eneya picked up the tale in my right.

"Oh, on visits she teaches us humans talks and acts. Humans are not-same."

I smiled and kissed her dusty grey wing, "You know, some humans say that about birds.

"Why are you two here?" I encouraged the birds to climb onto my arm so I could look at them.

They snuggled into each other.

"Our feathers felt magic two sunrises past." Eneya said.

"We recognised the pattern. It was you," Dash finished.

Their habit of completing each other's sentences threw me back to my teenage years when the two birds would hang around in my bedroom while I did my homework.

They had taken off to explore the country when I finished high school and I hadn't seen them since, probably because I had stopped practicing my magic.

"How long have you been back in town?"

They eyed each other, communicating in their own fashion.

Eneya answered, "About two cycles of seasons. We have flown over each season to see your little hatchlings."

I brushed my finger down her wing. "Speaking of hatchlings, have you any of your own this cycle?"

The birds had been a couple when I knew them and they'd already had several clutches of babies. Galahs mate for life and they had bonded mere months after hatching. If I had to guess, I would have placed them at about sixteen years old.

Eneya cheekily nipped my finger. "Many," she said,

"Our nest is past your bounds. Hatchlings fly soon."

A warmth spread through my heart.

"Do you need to get back to them?" I asked.

Dash tilted his head at me. "Yes, have you seeds?"

I shook my head at the cheeky little bird, even though I didn't expect any birds to become familiar with me as they had, I still kept a jar of sunflower seeds and tossed handfuls out for the local birds every now and again. I grabbed out a handful and placed the seeds and birds on the sink.

The seeds were quickly reduced to husks and the birds hopped up onto the windowsill to depart.

"Thanks, Clare," Eneya said.

"Yeah, thanks," Dash was moving rather slowly.

"Hey, you make sure you give that seed to the babies, you know too much is bad for you!"

"I know," the bird said as he flew away.

I smiled as my old friends flew away, happy to have them back in my life.

My joy quickly sank when the front door slammed open, and I remembered the other humans in my life, how was I going to be able to see my galahs without my family noticing anything strange?

Chapter Twelve

There are some questions in life that you must actively seek the answer for, and others that you really don't want to know. Examples of the latter include; 'what is that brown stuff on your face', followed closely by 'what manner of body fluid did you just wipe on my favourite shirt'?

"Amaya, shoes and socks please, it's time to go to school," I called.

It was the third time I had asked her. It had taken five attempts to get her to put on her jacket.

She waddled past me to the shoe box and pulled out a pair of sandals.

"Honey, you can't wear those shoes today, it's going to rain."

"But I want to!" she went from singing to screeching in ten seconds flat.

"I hate Tuesdays," I mumbled to myself.

Tuesdays were the day I started work at eight, so I had to hustle the kids out of the house and take them to Before School Care by 7:15AM. This meant rolling them out of bed and straight into the car before they had eaten any breakfast.

Hence the short tempers and my dislike of that particular weekday morning.

"Kaylee, honey, are you ready for school?"

She stomped around the corner of the passage with uneven footsteps. She glowered at me. One foot was full shoed, the other bare, an inside-out sock in one hand and a sneaker in the other.

"This sock is stupid."

Her butt thudded to the ground as she sat and wrestled with the sock, whining, "I can't do it."

"Let me help you."

She twisted away as I reached for the sock, "Nooooo!"

The word was drawn out to four syllables and three different notes. She had two more angry attempts to turn the sock through before she lost her temper, threw the 'stupid thing' in my direction and dissolved into a puddle of melodramatic tears on the floor.

I rolled my eyes skyward and silently asked myself if I would ever learn to wake up earlier and feed them on Tuesday mornings, but sometimes sleep deprived kids were just as tetchy as hungry ones. At least their school had sensible uniforms that still showed up looking good after they'd been slept in.

My nerves had started to fray by the time they were both appropriately shod.

I grabbed all of our bags and moved to the front door, "Alright kids, let's get out of here."

I nudged them out of the door ahead of me and pulled it shut, juggling the bags so I could lock the screen door.

"Come on Kaylee, get in the car, please." She had wandered off to look at the rose bushes.

"Look Mum, there's a spider web."

"That's great, it's probably eating the bugs that eat the rosebuds. Come and get in the car please, we have to go," the words were calm, but my exasperation was starting to show.

I tossed the bags in the boot and moved to Amaya's seat.

She was sorting through the DVDs in the centre console. How many thousands of times had we gotten in the car and they still didn't have the hang of 'get in the car, sit down, do up your buckle'. It drove me crazy.

"Mum, can we watch this one?" She asked.

"Not right now, we're only going to be in the car for a few minutes."

She dissolved into tears again as I wrestled her stocky little body into her car seat and did up her buckle. Kaylee still hadn't appeared when Amaya was finally subdued.

I shut Amaya's door and growled, "Kaylee, if you aren't in the car by the time I get to your door, I will throw out all of your favourite teddies."

The patter of little feet came up the driveway, "Not Munk munk?"

She scrambled to her car door just before I reached it.

"Yes, even Munk munk. Luckily, you made it just in time."

I buckled her up, closed the door and rested my forehead against it for a moment, letting my blood pressure drop back to normal before getting in the car.

"Oh, I'm so glad to have finally gotten through," the woman said after we had exchanged phone greetings, "I have been trying to get in touch to make an appointment for a few days now."

"I'm sorry to hear that," I kept my tone polite while rolling my eyes heavenward, "What was your name?"

She told me and I skimmed over the message book. Her name appeared three times, next to each was a note in my handwriting, 'left message'.

"Yes, I see. I've tried to call you back a couple of times, but the phone didn't connect, maybe it was off?"

"Oh no," she said, "It wouldn't have been off."

"Well, I did leave you a couple of messages, did you get those?"

"Oh no, I don't know how to use that," she said.

"Right. Okay. What can I do for you?"

I drew little stars on my notepad to keep my cool while I organised the appointment the woman needed.

I hung up and thumped my head down on the desk.

"One of those?" Amy asked from the doorway of my broom closet of an office.

"Yep."

Before I could get any further into it, the phone started to ring again.

I swore under my breath before picking up the phone.

"Oh, I think I was just speaking to you," the voice sent prickles into my neck, it was the woman again.

"Yes, that was me. Did you need to change that appointment?"

"No, I was just calling back to say that I checked and I didn't actually have any missed calls."

"No you wouldn't have, as I said, it didn't ring. Maybe you have incoming calls blocked?"

I couldn't believe the woman.

"No, I don't know how to do that."

I took a deep breath before speaking again.

"Maybe you were on the phone then?" I suggested.

"No, I'm hardly ever on it. I left all those messages and..."

My temper ran away like the dish ran away with the spoon – in a hurry and with flair.

"Listen, lady. You left messages, I called you back. Your phone didn't ring, so I left you a voicemail, which you told me you don't know how to retrieve. I did what you wanted me to do on the last call, but you felt the need to call me back and accuse me of lying about the call backs?"

"That's not what I was saying."

"Are you kidding me? Of course it was what you were saying. The accusation was at least implied from your words. If you leave messages for people and don't want to answer the phone, you should learn how to access your voicemail."

I was breathing hard when I finished my tirade. I steeled myself to respond to her next accusation, it took me a moment to realise that the other end of the line had gone silent.

My temper dissipated like liquid nitrogen on a hot frying pan and a flush of terror replaced my anger.

Oh, single bricks of lego. Lots of them. On their sides, or somehow on an angle so they poke right into your foot. What have I just done?

Losing my temper with my kids was one thing, and a

common enough occurrence, but I usually had the wherewithal to keep my collector cards together when talking to members of the public, or anyone not in my immediate family.

"Um, Ma'am?" I asked, "Are you still there?"

I heard a throat clear and acted quickly.

I cast out a psychic call and threw a magical tag on the woman.

A screech sounded in my mind and I shuddered.

"Dash? Turn it down will you?"

I put the phone handset down on the desk and cradled my forehead in my hands, closing my eyes to aid my concentration.

"Sorry, Clare. Difficult without practice, lucky you are that I spoke with north women. You should go, find friends maybe...."

"Dash, please, I need you to concentrate for a minute."

The chattering in my head quietened.

"I've tagged a lady, are you near her? She shouldn't be far from home."

There was silence for a moment, but a tickling sensation behind my nose assured me the connection was still open.

"I found the human. What shall I do to her?" His voice came through with a hint of malice and the image of him throwing gumnuts at her head popped into my mind.

"I don't want you to do anything to her. I just want you to fly up to her and be a beacon for me."

I got a hint of his subconscious chittering, it came through like whispers on the psychic connection.

"Fine," he said, "I'm at her nest."

I made sure the door to the little office was closed.

Many fictional limitations of magical modes of transport have been shown in books, TV shows and movies over the years, most of them are based on reality. The biggest problem with teleporting was navigation.

Working out where the heck you are going is difficult. You need to have a strong sense of direction and location

– knowing where you are is as important as knowing where you are going.

The other main issue is energy. It uses a lot of energy, physical and magical.

I didn't think I had enough energy to get myself to the woman, perform the magic I needed and then get back to the office. So I cheated.

"Are you ready?" I asked the bird.

He chittered and I performed the spell to occupy his body with him.

We were sitting on an outdoor chair on the back verandah of a house. A quick twist of our head gave me a dual impression of the yard.

It was tidy/not-wild.

Had a manicured lawn/inedible grass.

Had native plants/food.

I sensed that Dash was mentally cataloguing the location of the house and noting the seasons that each of the plants bloomed so he could come back when they were in season.

I mentally slapped myself and went back to the task at hand.

The woman was sitting in a chair opposite us, her phone to her ear. Her cheeks were flushed, but her eyes were staring directly at me, or, more accurately, at Dash. Dash's quick eye caught her firm grip on the pen, the quick throbbing of the vein at her neck, the beads of sweat appearing on her forehead.

If I didn't know better, I would think she was afraid of birds. I thought.

Humans fear birds? Dash asked.

Of course. Humans fear many things.

I hushed him and quickly worked my magic.

I sent a quick thought of thanks to Dash before gently detaching myself from his body and returning to my own.

I picked up the handset that was still resting on my desk.

"Are you there, Ma'am? The phone line seemed to go funny there for a minute, what were you saying?"

"Oh," her voice sounded tense, "I was just about to say that I didn't have any missed calls on my phone."

I breathed out a sigh. It worked; the woman had no recollection of my outburst.

"Oh, yes, that must be because the three times I called it went straight to voicemail, you must have been on the phone."

"Oh," she said. Her voice still sounded different to earlier.

"I'm sorry, but the practice policy is that we only try to call people back once per message. Otherwise we could spend all day trying to call people, only to discover they had called again and spoken to someone before we even started trying."

"I understand."

Her submissiveness was confusing given her earlier aggression.

"Is everything okay?"

"Yes, maybe, I don't know. It's just... I'm afraid of birds and there is currently a galah sitting on my arm."

The work day flew by after the hiccup and before I knew it, I was leaving to collect my dear little darlings from school.

Although Tuesday was hateful because of the heinously early start, it was also good because I got to finish early, pick the kids up when school finished and had an hour or so to relax before starting the rush of getting dinner ready and the kid's evening routine.

Yeah, who am I kidding, it wasn't relaxing, I had to break up a fight every five minutes because the children wanted to play with the same toy as each other, despite them have at least fifty thousand other toys to choose from.

But, the upside of Tuesday was that I got to touch base with my kids teachers and see how they were going. The majority of the time, the teachers didn't have anything to say, it was just covering how they are SO much better behaved for their teachers than they are for me.

I collected Amaya from her class and moved up to Kaylee's.

Kaylee's teacher saw me coming down the corridor and she gestured at me.

"Oh, Clare, I'm glad I've caught you." Words to strike fear into any parent's heart, "Can I have a quick word?"

The smile on her face suggested I was about to be embarrassed, I felt my cheeks reddening in anticipation.

"Oh, sure. Girls, would you like to go play on the playground for a minute?"

They shrieked, slipped their bags off their shoulders and ran off.

"Take your bags!" My cry was in vain, they were gone.

I rolled my eyes and picked up their school bags, throwing one on each shoulder.

"I'll take them then."

I followed the teacher, Miss Mason, into the classroom. She had moved over to her desk and picked up a piece of paper which she held to her chest as she walked back to me. A spark in her eye suggested humour.

"She's not in trouble, I just thought you might get a laugh out of this."

Strangely, my heart sank further at her words.

"Oh?" I hedged.

"So, the other day were talking about things that we like to do and things we like to play with and we talked about how different people like to play with different things. I asked the kids to draw pictures of things that the people in their family liked to play with and this is what Kaylee gave me."

Predictably, Munk Munk featured next to Kaylee's name. A Gruffalo and a computer were drawn and labelled with 'Amaya' and 'Daddy' respectively and then there was mine.

The shape of the drawing could only be described as phallic. A hot pink, penis shape was drawn next to 'Mummy'.

"Oh!" I said, scouring my mind as to what on earth the child had drawn, then it got worse.

"When I asked her what that was, she said it was something you kept in your bedroom and it shakes and it makes you go 'oooohhhh'."

My eyes popped wider as the teacher started giggling.

"It's not a vibrator!" I blurted, sudden realisation striking me, "It's a muscle massage bar, I roll it under my shoulders when my muscles get tight. I promise you, it is not a vibrator! I don't keep those where the kids could get their hands on it, besides, that isn't pink, it's...."

I trailed off as the teacher's laughter abruptly stopped and I realised that I had said too much.

"Just to be clear," she said, suppressed laughter showing itself as a smile, "I never thought it was a, one of those... I just thought you'd get a laugh out of the drawing. I asked Kaylee to draw another picture where she drew a book for you because you like to read."

She thrust the offending piece of paper at me, "You can take this one home and show your husband."

Yeah, I would not be showing him that. No way in the Shopkins pot!

My cheeks felt hot enough to start a fire, I forced a laugh, "Yeah, that is funny."

She smiled at me.

"Well, have a good night!" I scurried to the door.

"You too, Clare," her voice followed me as I raced to the playground to collect my children and take myself closer to my much needed wine.

"Oh, by the way," she called.

I turned back and made embarrassed eye contact.

"There's been a couple of cases of headlice in the class this week, it might pay to check the girl's hair."

Oh, because this day just couldn't get any worse.

Chapter Thirteen

If you're going to mop yourself into a corner, make sure it's one with a comfy chair and snacks.

It was a stunning day.

The weather had turned it on and we were out enjoying the sunshine.

The temperature was perfect, a gentle breeze cooled my skin and the sun shone through the trees in a way often used for scenes of reminiscence in movies.

Basically, it was the sort of weather that made me wonder when the other shoe would drop, when the impending disaster would occur, and made me feel as though I was not long for this world.

I know, the last sounds melodramatic, but there are times when everything is just so perfect and glorious that I'm sure that I'm not meant to be here to enjoy it for long. That these days are so amazing - it must be a gift I've been given because the end of my days is nigh.

With these conflicting emotions – wonder and amazement warring with melancholy and fear – we packed a picnic and met Trin, Sian and Arlo at the park.

We brought the husbands to offload the parenting.

Trin and I sat on the picnic rug drinking coffee out of reusable cups (we decided it was too early to drink alcohol in public, plus the playground was a dry zone). Picnic food was packed and ready to eat – homemade goodies and lunch on Trin's side, whatever crap I'd picked up from the supermarket on mine – and we were taking the opportunity to relax while the boys had the con.

"I can't believe he did that to you," I said, "Just not show up at home like that. He's normally so good at letting you know his plans."

"I know! It's not likely I normally mind when he goes out, I just want forewarning so I can prepare myself. I run the whole evening differently when I'm home alone."

"Yeah, but you were waiting to eat dinner with him, that's just so rude."

Our husband bashing was interrupted by a shriek.

Trin sat up straight and peered at the playground.

"Don't worry," I said, "It's mine."

I had immediately recognised Amaya's voice. "Michael should get her."

The noise grew louder and Trin's husband, Frank, deposited Amaya in my lap.

I pulled her close and patted her back while my temper bubbled.

"Where's Michael?" I asked Frank.

"Not sure," he said.

Eventually, Amaya calmed enough to tell me what was wrong.

Through her sobs, I worked out that she had fallen off the spinner.

"Okay, okay," I soothed, "Did you hurt yourself or scare yourself?"

"Hurt myself and scared myself."

"Where did you hurt yourself?"

She proceeded to point to areas of her body which I kissed better. She giggled when I kissed the imaginary ache on her bottom and happily wandered off.

Michael plonked himself down on the rug, almost sitting on my coffee. I wrenched the cup of precious brew to safety.

"What happened to Amaya?" Michael asked.

"She fell off the twisty stick thing, why weren't you there to comfort her?" I growled.

He leaned back and held his hands up in defence, "I had to take Kaylee to the toilet. Of course I heard Amaya cry, but I wanted to make sure Kaylee didn't get stolen by the goblin king, so I stayed with her."

"Fine," I said.

I knew it wasn't his fault, but I wasn't ready to concede that I had been wrong in accusing him of neglecting his duty. I was pointlessly peeved at having to parent in that particular moment.

Silence hung heavy between us for a moment until Trin cleared her throat.

I had almost forgotten she was there.

"So," she said, "how about that local sporting team?"

"Which one?" Frank asked as her re-joined us.

"Any of them," Trin met Frank's eyes and I saw her give him a look.

"Why does the golfer carry two shirts?"

Trin obliged him, "I don't know, why?"

"In case he gets a hole in one!"

We all laughed, although Michael's laugh sounded strange and mine was faked.

My stomach rumbled, loudly.

"I guess it must be time for lunch!" Trin said, "Will you guys fetch the children, we'll lay it out."

Michael and Frank loped off across the park to round up the offspring and Trin fixed me with a critical look.

"What?" I asked, pausing the unpacking of my picnic bag.

"Are you okay?" She asked.

"Me? Of course I'm okay, I'm always okay," I thought about her question from a different angle, "Why wouldn't I be?"

"It's just," she paused, "you've been a little short tempered lately, a little off. More... jaded than you usually are."

"No, I haven't. Have I?"

She nodded with a grimace. "A little. And normally you would be the first to spring up to go and help your kid if they were crying, not berating Michael for not doing it."

I groaned. "Ugh, I guess you're right. I don't know what it is. I think I'm just tired, and a little grumpy. Maybe I'm about to get my period."

Trin shrugged, "I think it's more than that. You're tired?"

"Yeah, I haven't been sleeping that well for the past few nights, plus it's the middle of the term now, we've been running around like mad things for weeks. And there's always something else that pops up just when you think you've gotten on top of it."

"Hmmm," Trin agreed as she set her homemade, low sugar, half carb, wholemeal brownie slice on the blanket.

I loved Trin, but sometimes she fed my inferiority complex.

She sat up and looked at me. "You seem a little pale. Maybe you need your iron levels checked?"

I shrugged, "Yeah, maybe. I'll get one of the Docs at work to do me up a form next week."

Just another thing added to my mother load.

I packed the remainder of our picnic into our bags, stuffing the plastic bags from our supermarket fare inside each other to go in the plastic recycling when we got home.

Michael tended to laugh when he saw me packing all the soft plastics inside each other.

"Why do you even bother?" he would ask, "You never remember to take them with you to the supermarket anyway."

Just thinking about the criticism made my stomach clench. It was like he didn't even care about what state we would leave the planet in for our children, the actions we would need to take to correct the damage of our forebears and leave the place habitable for those who come after.

Let future Michael think about future Michael's problems. Ugh.

Trin took off to play with the kids and I settled back to look at the sky.

The shouts and laughter of the kids and parents reached me, but didn't bring a smile to my face as it usually would.

"You're just tired," I told myself, "that's all."

I watched the leaves wave in the breeze, something which usually calmed me, but a low buzzing in the back of my head stopped me from being able to relax. I was sure I could remember days where watching the children play together would make me smile and fill me with a soul-deep warmth, but lately I just wasn't feeling it.

My husband just tended to irritate me when he gave me cuddles and I felt like I was begrudging the children the love they deserved.

I sighed and noticed that the buzzing was turning into another headache. I'd suffered so many lately, I wish I knew the cause. I pondered on it as it grew, trying to work out if there was a pattern to the aching, but nothing came to mind.

Maybe it was a brain tumour.

My stomach lurched and my intestines roiled at the thought.

It would make sense, I told myself.

My thoughts spiralled as I wondered what Michael and the children would do without me. The thoughts fit the melancholy feel of the day, like the golden days had passed me and a tumult lay ahead.

It would be so awful for the children to see me fading like that. All pale and having lost all my hair. I won't be able to do anything much with them in the last few months, if I even get that long from now.

The fingers of my right hand tensed and twitched, my headaches always started on the right hand side, maybe the twitching was a further symptom.

My heart beat a rapid tattoo and my chest clenched around it. Pain rose as a vice tightened around my chest.

The world as I knew it was ending and my family and friends were metres away, oblivious to it all.

The tension rose and just as I thought the pressure would cause me to scream, a leaf fell on my face.

The brush of the dry gum leaf across my face drew me partially back from the brink of my panic.

I huffed breath out of my nose and brushed away the distraction.

My mind immediately sank back into panic mode. I felt my bowels growl insistently, a warning twinge that a trip to the bathroom would be needed soon. Sweat started soaking through the fabric of my shirt from my armpits.

A small gumnut hit me and nearly went up my nose, startling me upright to wipe my face and blow air sharply through my nose.

I looked up at the canopy of leaves overhead, but couldn't spy anything.

"Cheech," the quiet bird call drew my attention to an overhanging branch.

Eneya sat above me, a small branch of leaves in her beak. As I watched, she tossed her head and let it go.

The little bouquet of leaves flurried down toward me, landing in my lap.

I narrowed my eyes at her, "What are you up to, you cheeky thing?"

"Cheech, cheech," she said, choosing not to speak words I could understand.

I pulled the branch from my lap and tossed it aside. I stretched when I stood to make my way to the bathroom. I noticed that my shoulders were tight and rolled them a few times to release the tension. When I pulled my neck to the side, it released my headache.

"Muscular!" I laughed, "It's a muscular headache!"

Suddenly I realised that my moment of panic had been crazy, of course I didn't have a brain tumour. Why had I driven myself into such a frenzy like that?

I cast a smile at Michael, standing at the edge of the playground. He lifted his chin and threw me a kiss.

I breathed out and released the tension, but kept walking to the bathroom, the panic may have subsided, but the gastrointestinal symptoms had not.

As I had predicted, Michael busted me pulling the plastic bags out of the picnic basket when we got home. He walked into the kitchen at a very inopportune moment.

"Did you really bring that rubbish home with you?" he asked.

I jumped straight to the defensive, "Yes. Don't you realise how much plastic goes into landfill each year? By the time our children have children half the planet will be covered in rubbish dumps!"

"Hardly," Michael said, "Don't you know how long humans have lived on this planet already? I hardly think the changes in the next twenty years will be quite as drastic as you imagine."

I tried to keep a lid on my temper, "There you go discounting my opinion again. Of course I know humans have been on Earth for hundreds of thousands of years, but our practices have changed so drastically in the last two hundred years! Don't you realise that there was practically no rubbish aside from organic waste until relatively recently in our timeline?"

Michael opened his mouth to interrupt, but the lid on the kettle of my temper had well and truly blown and l was now boiling away unchecked.

"Have you heard of the great pacific garbage patch? They estimate the size of the patch to be between the size of New South Wales to twice the size of Australia. A study last year showed eighty per cent of all the plastic ever created is no longer in use. That's over six billion tonnes! And over five billion is waste, either in dumps or littered somewhere. How are future generations going to survive?

"And that's only the scenario around plastic waste, don't get me started on carbon pollution and global warming."

Michael had crossed the room when I was in the middle of my tirade. He now stood before me and gently took the plastic bags from my hand. Apparently I'd been waving them about.

"Okay," Michael said slowly, "I won't mention global warming."

He said this in the tone people usually reserve for the line "Don't mention the war."

"Don't patronise me."

"I wouldn't," he said, "there just seems to be so many other things for you to worry about, and you choose to worry about the Pacific trash land."

"It's the Great Pacific Garbage Patch. If you're going to ridicule me, at least use the correct nomenclature."

His eyes crinkled in the corners, but his mouth did not betray his amusement.

I didn't know whether to punch him in the chest for his insolence or kiss him for putting up with my crazy.

"Ugh," I settled for a flat handed press to his chest, "go away."

He pressed a quick kiss to my lips and ran away before I could make him do any housework.

I retrieved the plastic bags from the bench and stuffed them into the bag I kept next to the bin. No matter how I tried, what points I used, he still didn't see my point on environmental issues.

He had the view that if it was what everyone else did, why shouldn't we? Why should we put so much effort into putting the kids' sandwiches into containers instead of using plastic bags or cling wrap like our parents did?

The old conversation rolled through my mind as I clattered around the kitchen, moving from unpacking lunch to preparing dinner.

"But it's such a pain to wash all these containers," he would complain.

We would argue, but in the end I packed the lunchboxes, so, generally speaking, there was no cling wrap in sight.

Sometimes I would mention my plastic concerns to other parents. A particularly awkward exchange occurred at a party for one of Kaylee's friends a few months earlier.

I had admired that, although the party had taken place at a playground, the host had used platters and containers to serve the food and given out cake on serviettes rather than using plastic plates.

Another parent had not quite agreed with my views.

"I don't know why she didn't just serve the cake on plates; it's really awkward to eat."

I was standing behind the woman who was speaking to another parent.

I rolled my eyes and tried to ignore them, what was that old saying? 'Eavesdroppers only hear ill of themselves'?

"I bet she is the sort of mother who doesn't use zip-lock bags."

The first mother turned to the second, "What do you mean?"

The second groaned. "You know, one of the mums who only uses BPA-free containers to pack their organic, chemical free lunches for their little angels."

I didn't need to see the woman's face to know a smirk adorned it.

I couldn't stay silent in the face of such slander against another mother, even though I didn't know the birthday girl's mother very well.

I wasn't normally one to go out of my way to start a fight, but Aunt Flo was on her way and I was itching to relieve some hormonal tension.

"Oh," I said, stepping forward, "What's wrong with the organic food? Have they found Escherichia coli in the bean sprouts again?"

Yes, I said Escherichia coli instead of E.coli like most people would, it's a fun word to say.

Escherichia- Esh-err-ish-ee-uh.

The two women looked at me blankly.

"Because that is the only reason I can think of for shaming people for buying organic produce. As far as I see it, if someone wants to pay more money for smaller vegetables, it's completely their call. I wish I could avoid chemicals on all of our food, but unfortunately my vegetable garden isn't quite producing enough to feed the whole family."

My vegetable garden wasn't producing enough to feed an ant. It was non-existent, except for the purpose of the argument.

The two women stared at me. The first studied me like I was one of those jigsaw puzzles with no edge pieces.

I continued, "But, I do also avoid zip-lock bags, and most single use plastics as a rule. I see no reason to add to the plastic burden, so most of my kids lunches are packed in containers which are BPA-free as that is basically industry standard since all those pesky articles were written in the medical journals."

The first woman heard a point she could argue.

"I bet you use a dishwasher to wash them though. Don't you realise how many chemicals you release into the environment with the dishwashing powder?"

"A heck of a lot less than your plastic bags do."

If I had held a glass of wine I would have sipped it to add gravitas. As it was I settled for taking an exorbitantly large bite of chocolate cake.

Which meant I left myself wide open for counter attack.

"That may be so." I took her shark-like smile as a warning. If I was a fish every cell in my body would have been fighting to swim away. "But did you know that children in a house where the dishwasher is used are forty per cent more likely to have immune disorders? That covers both Asthma and Eczema, just so you know."

The two women skewered me with a glare and walked away.

Instead of making the women rethink being judgemental cats, I'd been left feeling guilty about cleaning my dishes. Brilliant.

"Yeah, well, I guess everyone is entitled to be ignorant." My retort had fallen an empty air, I had thought of it several minutes after the women had left.

I hated how often that happened. I can't count how many times I've thought of the perfect witty retort or comeback when it will no longer hold relevance.

Just the general story of my life, all the important knowledge and realisations come way after they would have been helpful.

Chapter Fourteen

Denial is more than just a river in Egypt.

The work week rolled around again and I was on my way to make my second coffee when I remembered the promise I'd made to Trin.

"I need to get my iron levels checked." I told my empty office.

I opened up the program showing appointments and skimmed down to see if any of the doctors were free.

"Ahaha!"

Room four, Doctor Murray had ten minutes to his next appointment, and it was a regular patient who was habitually late.

I stepped out of my little office and walked down the corridor to the consulting rooms. The door to Doctor Murray's room was closed and I hesitated for a moment.

What if he's on the phone? What if he's writing up notes on a patient? Surely my iron levels weren't worth interrupting him?

I paused outside the door, my heart thundering and armpits dampening with my indecision.

Quick tapping footsteps sounded around the corner and another doctor appeared.

"Clare," she looked at me, her head cocked to one side, "Are you ok? You look pale."

I stared at her like Dash when I'd busted him with his head in the sunflower seed jar.

"Doctor Imra. I'm fine," I rushed up a lie, "I just had some results to give Doctor Murray."

She pointed at my empty hands.

"I already gave them to him. I was just waiting for..."

Doctor Imra held up her hand in the universal sign for 'stop talking'.

"Clare, why don't you come in here with me for a minute?"

She opened the door to her consulting room and gestured me in.

I trudged to the patient chair next to her desk and she closed the door. I ran my thumb over each of my fingernails as I waited for her to sit.

Right thumb over left thumb nail, index finger, central finger, ring finger, pinkie. I swapped thumbs and repeated the process on the other hand.

"Clare," Doctor Imra's middle eastern accent was rich and soothing, "Why don't you tell me what's bothering you?"

"Well," a sudden wall barred me from saying my worries aloud, *I'm only asking for a stupid blood test, what's the fuss about?* I repeated the process with my fingernails and exhaled slowly. "I have been feeling a bit tired lately, and my friend was worried about me, so she said I should get my iron levels checked."

Whew, that wasn't so bad.

"Do you usually have trouble with your iron levels?"

I wrinkled my brow, "No, not usually. My iron is usually in the upper end of the normal range."

"Hmm," she said, "let me check your blood pressure."

I sat still while she put the cuff around my arm and it inflated.

"How are the kids?" she smiled as she asked.

"Oh, you know, they drive me crazy most of the time and they certainly keep me busy!"

I stopped talking while the cuff inflated and measured.

The instrument beeped.

"That's pretty much perfect," Doctor Imra said absently, "Do you get much time to do things for yourself, on your own?"

I was puzzled by the topic change, "I guess, a little? A friend asked me to crochet a baby blanket for her, she's only fifteen weeks pregnant now, so I should be able to have it done by the time she has the baby."

I gave a dry laugh.

"But that's not really you time then, is it? Making something for someone?" she asked gently. She switched to a brisk tone, "Tell me your normal daily routine."

It was an order, not a question.

"Well, I get up around 6:00. I have a shower and breakfast, then I get the kids lunches ready. By the time that's done, the kids are up and it's time for them to have breakfast and get dressed."

My alarm goes off at six, I corrected the story in my head, *I snooze it for at least twenty minutes, so that by the time I get in the shower I only have time for the merest of splashes and wiping of the particularly stinky bits. Not that I actually stick to that time limit. I scoff down a couple of pieces of toast while making the lunchboxes just after seven. The kids come down at 7:30, which is about an hour before we leave home and should, theoretically, be enough time to get them to eat a bowl of cereal and change their clothes. Theoretically. In practice, I spend forty five minutes reminding Amaya that she needs to eat her toast, only to discover that she's only eaten half a slice – but not the crusts – five minutes before we have to leave.*

Then there's five frantic minutes of me shouting Amaya's clothes onto her, putting her toast on a plastic plate so she can finish it in the car, hoping that Kaylee has sorted herself, and finally hitting the road to school only to realise that I left Amaya's toast on the bench.

"That's a busy morning," Doctor Imra said about my theoretical morning routine, "Would you say that is usually a stressful time of day?"

I considered the question. *This morning I let my daughter eat a lollipop for breakfast because it was the only way to get her in the car and stop the screaming.*

I tried to give a non-committal shrug, "I guess it can

be."

99.999999999 per cent of the time.

Her eyes narrowed, but I didn't cave under the weight of her disbelief.

"And the kids? Are they usually happy to go to school?"

"Yeah," I said, "They love school."

That, at least, was the truth. They had gone through their rough patches, but at the moment, they were both going into class without emotionally blackmailing me.

"And once they're at school, what do you do?"

"I come to work, at least on four days out of five," I smiled, "I'm lucky, I don't have to work full time."

Lucky. Because I only have to work part time to keep a roof over our heads while working every other hour of the day to keep the house running smoothly *eyeroll*.

"What time do you normally finish?"

"Four. My kids go to out of school hours care for a bit, so I pick them up and head home for the dinner, homework, bathtime rush."

Ah bathtime, where the girls turn into a cacophony of children.

"So," Doctor Imra probed gently, "When do you get time to do something on your own, just for you?"

"Well, I do stuff on my phone in the morning." The doctor raised her brows at me, "I have some puzzles that I do every day."

The half an hour spent on social media, email and puzzles after my early morning alarm was usually the cause of my perpetual morning rush.

She nodded, "What about exercise or getting out of the house?"

"We take the kids to parks and stuff on weekends, but I don't usually know what to do then. I'm not fit enough to run around, so I usually just sit and play more games on my phone."

"Would you say you sleep well?"

The question threw me and I felt my brow wrinkle, "What are you getting at?"

"Just bear with me another few minutes," She turned to her computer and opened a browser window.

I couldn't see what she was doing but she gestured me over to her desk a minute later.

"Clare," her steady gaze pierced me, "I want you to fill in this survey for me, and I want you to be completely honest. With me, and with yourself."

My mouth went dry and my gut clenched as I sat in the computer chair.

The header at the top of the page read 'Anxiety and Depression Checklist'.

No, I can't be depressed! People only get depression if something awful has happened to them, I'm just stressed.

"Clare," Doctor Imra prompted.

I had been staring blankly at the screen

"But I can't be depressed. No one in my family has died recently, the kids are healthy, my husband helps out around the house. I've seen so many people in worse situations...."

Doctor Imra held out a hand to cut me off. "This isn't about other people, Clare. This is about you and I would like you to complete the survey for me."

I rolled my eyes and turned back to the computer. I was faced with a series of questions with multiple choice answers - 'None of the time', 'A little of the time', 'Some of the time', 'Most of the time', or 'All of the time'. The disclaimer at the top of the survey said 'This simple checklist aims to measure whether you may have been affected by depression and anxiety during the past four weeks. The higher your score, the more likely you are to be experiencing depression and/or anxiety.'

Hooray. I steeled myself and started on the list.

'About how often did you feel tired out for no good reason?' Well, I'm always tired, but that's usually just from chasing every one and thinking about all the things I have to do. When I thought about all the neglected housework because I was so bone-tired I just couldn't bring myself to do it... I ticked the box for 'Most of the time.'

'About how often did you feel nervous?' I gave that a

'Some of the time'

'About how often did you feel so nervous nothing could calm you down?' I thought about the other night when I was worrying about the teenager who had gone missing and I had to play Sudoku to get to sleep. 'Some of the time.'

'About how often did you feel hopeless?' What, like I am a hopeless mother or that there isn't any hope in the world? 'None of the time.'

'About how often did you feel restless of fidgety?' I noticed that my leg was bouncing when I read this one. I generally have trouble sitting down, I feel like I should be doing something, and then if I'm not doing something, I feel guilty about it. 'Most of the time' for that one.

'About how often did you feel so restless you could not sit still?' I guess the answer for that one was in the previous. 'Most of the time'.

'About how often did you feel depressed?' Well, I'm not depressed. 'None of the time'.

'About how often did you feel that everything was an effort?' Well, parenting isn't exactly effortless. 'Most of the time'.

'About how often did you feel so sad that nothing could cheer you up?' That one's pretty easy. I went to click 'none of the time' and then I thought harder. There were times when I had felt sad and not even the kids crazy antics cheered me. Like when they had cut my hair, but they had just cut my hair, surely no-one would expect me to be turning cartwheels around the neighbourhood after that? 'A little of the time' then.

Last question.

'About how often did you feel worthless?' Well that one stung. My eyes pricked. There were times when I felt that my efforts weren't enough, that I wasn't providing well enough for my family. That I wasn't good enough for them. That was about the same as feeling worthless wasn't it? 'Some of the time'

I answered the last question and moved away from the computer so Doctor Imra could do whatever she needed to.

I avoided her eyes, but she put her hand on my shoulder and squeezed. Her eyes held sympathy and it was all I could do to keep those stupid pricking tears at bay.

My fingers prickled too. Part of me must have felt that the tears were caused by some form of threat and the magic was an instinctive defence.

"Okay," said Doctor Imra, "I've got that result through and it looks like there's a chance you might currently be struggling with some depression or anxiety. There is another questionnaire I would like you to complete."

She clicked another tab open on the computer.

When I moved back to the computer the heading said 'Anxiety checklist'.

I read the instructions.

'Please consider the following questions and rate how true each one is in relation to how you have been feeling lately (i.e. over the last two weeks) compared to how you usually or normally feel.' This time there were only four possible answers - 'Not at all', 'Several days', 'More than half the days', or 'Nearly every day'.

'Feeling nervous, anxious or on edge?' Nervous, well, not really. Anxious, what did that even mean really? I guessed it was about worry. I was probably a bit of a worrier. I ticked the 'More than half the days' box.

'Not being able to stop or control worrying'. I guessed 'Several days' for this one.

'Worrying too much about different things?' How much worry was too much though? I asked Dr Imra.

"Generally," she said, "If worry breaks through your other thoughts, if it interferes with what you are doing, then it is too much. Do you ever find you can't focus on something because you are worrying?"

I nodded, I guess it was 'More than half the days' box for that one.

'Trouble relaxing'. Ha! What is relaxing? I don't think I've felt relaxed since before Kaylee was born! 'Nearly every day'.

'Being so restless it's hard to sit still'. Well, that's

84

basically the same as the question on the last survey, but worded slightly differently. 'Nearly every day' seemed to fit best as I rarely managed to sit down without doing something.

'Being easily annoyed or irritable'. Well, I have children, they are annoying and irritating, so... Once again I had to stop and think. How many mums did I see at school drop-off who did seem to have their shit together? How many of them had already lost their shit at their kids five times before the first bell? People never really reveal their emotional state to semi-strangers though.

I thought about Trin. Her kids were easily as annoying as mine, and I had lost my cool in front of her several times, but I had never seen her raise her voice. Maybe I was more easily aggravated.

I thought again of our trip the park on the weekend. I had lost my cool at Michael when he was taking care of Kaylee and I had to see to Amaya. Plus there was that little outburst to the lady on the phone. 'More than half the days'?

'Feeling afraid as if something awful might happen'. Well that was pretty much what I had felt at the park the other day wasn't it? How often *did* I feel like that though? I hedged my bets and chose 'More than half the days'.

I scanned over the questions and responses again, nodded and let Doctor Imra back to her computer.

She clicked for the results and turned back to me.

I watched her cross her legs at the knee – *She should know that's bad for her, she'll end up with varicose veins* - she twined her fingers together and sat them on her knee.

"So, Clare," she had shifted back to her soothing voice now, like I was a startled kitten, "The results of that questionnaire show you might be suffering from some anxiety. What I want to do is take you through some questions so I can make you a mental health care plan, this will allow you to see a psychologist for six visits at the cost of the government. There won't be any cost to you, okay?"

Yeah, okay, no cost, but crikey, when was I going to be able to fit that in? And what did 'Anxiety' even mean, that I worry too much? But aren't mothers meant to worry? We're always meant to be thinking about our children's care, their health, their teeth, so who was to say it wasn't just worry?

I murmured the last question, but Doctor Imra heard me.

"Clare," her voice was still velvet, "You were going to see Doctor Murray for something, would you tell me again what that was?"

"My friend told me I seemed tired, and maybe a bit grumpier than usual. She said I'd been acting strange. I thought maybe low iron would explain it. Could low iron make me worried too?"

I was clutching at straws. I didn't want to have anxiety. That was a mental health condition. I didn't want to be a sufferer of a mental health condition. Wouldn't that make it hard to get life insurance? *Man, I really should get life insurance. What if I die and we don't have it? What would happen to the house? The kids?*

"Clare?" A hand waved in front of my face. I focussed back on the Doctor, "I've read that iron deficiency doesn't *cause* anxiety, but it can make symptoms worse. If you like, I can arrange a blood test for you?"

"Yes, thank you," I said. "And thank you for caring enough to make me do the survey; I'm sure it's not that bad though, it's probably just my iron."

Her eyes narrowed and she held out the pathology form. "Alright, here's the deal – you do this test and if it comes back low, I'll give you some iron tablets and we'll be square. If it comes back in the normal range though, you'll come back to see me, and we'll do a mental health care plan."

"Deal."

I shook her hand and left the room.

Chapter Fifteen

I just had the perfect sentence, and now it's gone.
True story.

I decided not to tell Michael about my visit with Doctor Imra. I didn't want to cause him to worry more than usual and put him on the radar for anxiety too, ha!

I thought about my conversation with the good doctor as I cooked dinner that night.

I don't have anxiety. I told myself as the frying onions stung my eyes. I stirred more violently than usual.

I had a friend from Uni, Owen, who used to have panic attacks in the weeks leading up to exams. I found him hiding in the corner of the library a few times.

"I can't do it, Clare," he would say, talking between great, gulping breaths as he clutched at his chest. "None of it makes sense. I can't get the numbers right, I'm going to fail, I know I am."

At twenty-one, the sight of him in such distress terrified me. His eyes were wild, his hands held a white-knuckle grip on his knees and he tapped his toes.

Eventually, he calmed down and started breathing normally; I was on the verge of calling an ambulance for him though.

"What the hell was that?" I asked him.

"I think it was a panic attack," he said, "I'm sorry you had to see that, I'm normally tough enough to not do that in public."

"In public? How often do you have them? When did it start?" I was sitting next to him and pushed up close to share our body warmth.

"That was my fourth, I think," he said, his cheeks were now flushed with embarrassment, "I had the first attack three weeks ago, I thought I was having a heart attack. I went to see the counsellor and he told me it was a panic attack. He gave me some tips about how to get over them, but sometimes it takes me a few minutes to remember."

"What does it feel like? How does it happen?" I asked, curious now the scare had passed.

"It starts with a thought, it's usually about study or exams," we were finishing up our first semester of the second year of our accounting degrees, "I think 'I've been studying so hard, but I can't remember any of it.' I won't remember the right sums for calculating compound interest or something and then I'll fail. I'll fail all of my subjects and they won't let me come back next semester and then I'll never get a job because I'm so terrible at maths and I'll end up homeless living under the bridge over the Torrens at Frome Road."

I couldn't help myself, I laughed, "But that's crazy!"

"No," he said, "it's irrational. I know that most of the exams are only worth a third of my grade and I have scored well on all the essays and tests throughout the semester. Even if I did fail the exam, I know I would be offered a supplementary. If worse came to worse I could even change degrees, but none of that comes to mind while I'm having a panic attack."

"But... Why the bridge under Frome Road?"

He shrugged, "No idea, I guess it came to mind at some point and stuck."

I reached over, grabbed his hand and squeezed it in mine, "Are you okay now?"

He held out his hand, "Still a little shaky, but I'll be okay. The counsellor taught me some tricks to calm down."

I cocked my head, "What sort of tricks?"

"One is to focus on breathing, but then there is a whole process with your senses. She said you find five things you can see, four things you can hear, three things you can feel, two things you can smell and one thing you can taste."

"So you did that then?"

He smiled weakly, "Yeah. I saw the books, my bag, my shoelaces, the lights, your hair. I heard footsteps in the next aisle, the buzz of the light, the water in the pipes overhead, your voice. I could feel my shoes on my feet, my phone in my pocket and your hand on my shoulder. I could smell my deodorant and your perfume. I could taste remnants of my tuna sandwich for lunch."

I laughed at the last part, it relieved the tension. I had felt butterflies in my stomach as he so earnestly told all the things he'd noticed about me. Being the almost sole focus of someone's attention was intoxicating, I discovered.

Plus, I was drawn to him like I would have been drawn to a wounded animal, seeing him so exposed made me want to nurture him.

I closed my eyes and turned my face toward him.

"Uh, Clare," he whispered, "What are you doing?"

I quickly changed course and placed a peck on his cheek.

"Just kissing you. Geez, you act like I'm going to give you girl germs."

"Maybe you are."

After the first time, Owen would text me if he needed help with the panic attacks and we became proper friends. There were a few other moments that held the magic of an almost liaison, but we never hooked up.

We are still in touch though, mainly by liking pictures of each other's kids on Facebook; he has a two-year-old son with his partner, Bea.

Maybe I could talk to him about my 'anxiety'. Not yet though, it was probably just my iron levels, no need to worry him about it yet.

Or was there a need to worry about it? Maybe the worrying was just the early phases of an anxiety disorder, maybe they would build up, maybe they worsened.

What if I did end up as the sort of person who would curl up in a ball in the corner and never move, paralysed by fear? What sort of parent would I be then? Definitely a hopeless one.

My breathing came faster and I realised that my eyes were watering. *Just from the onions, I'm not crying.*

I am not a crier.

I am not crying!

Despite my insistent denial, I eventually had to accept that the tears running down my cheeks were not caused by the chemical reactions of my frying onions.

My heart was pounding, my stomach was churning and my thoughts were a maelstrom.

Where are the kids? What if they come in and see me like this, will they think I'm crazy? What will Michael think? Maybe he'll have me hospitalised? What if they never let me out?

Finally, Owen's voice came through, the distant memory weak, but there, "Five things you can see, four things you can hear, three things you can feel, two things you can smell and one thing you can taste."

I can see the frying pan (are the onions burning?), the kettle, the swingset (covered in spiderwebs, I should clean those so the kids don't get bitten), the table, the dishwasher (needs to be emptied). The kids playing (not hairdressers again I hope), the tv (on with no-one watching it, no doubt) the gas, the hot water system. My wedding bands (loose as always), the blisters on my little toes rubbing in my shoes, the hook of my bra scratching my back. I can smell the coffee I haven't drunk yet, the frying onions. I can taste, what can I taste? The muck of my post-nasal drip from my crying jag (ugh).

The tears had stopped but I still felt like the room was spinning around me and staying upright was a struggle. I turned the gas off and moved the pan so I didn't burn the dinner and took a deep breath before starting the exercise again. I had probably done it wrong. I tried to only notice the items this time and can the thoughts about them.

I see the kitchen cupboards, my dining chair, my favourite mug (full of delicious coffee for me to drink), the kids swingset (where they have fun) and a block of chocolate (my favourite – black forest). I can hear happy children, birds outside, a lawnmower (who mows their lawns on a weeknight?) and my windchimes. I can feel my wedding bands (symbols of my commitment to Michael and his to me), my comfy pants hugging my bum, the ponytail holding my hair back. I can smell the onions frying and the flowers on the table. I can taste the dinner I am going to have ready soon.

I breathed out slowly, the panic seemed to have subsided, but I was exhausted, wrung out from the chemicals running through my system. I picked up my favourite mug and took a sip of my cold coffee, washed away my worries and got back to work.

"You've been quiet today," Michael said as he curved his body around mine on the sofa that night.

I stretched my legs out onto the ottoman and absorbed the blissful peace of the house.

"Kids are both in bed?" I asked, ignoring his comment.

"Tucked in with the night light on."

"How many unicorns does Amaya have with her tonight?" I smiled.

"I think four, but that's only what she was cuddling, who knows how many others were tucked into bed with her."

He pressed a kiss to the crown of my head.

"This afternoon she was dressed in all unicorns. Unicorn t-shirt, pants, skirt, socks, headband. I wouldn't be surprised if she was even wearing unicorn knickers. Then she put on a cape and called herself 'Super Unicorn'."

I could feel him shake his head and his chest shook from his soft laugh, "That kid cracks me up."

I fell silent and snuggled for a few minutes before my idleness got to me.

"Where are you going?" Michael asked.

"Just to get my crochet."

I fetched the bag and sat next to him, unable to

snuggle now as I needed my hooking arm free.

"Shall I put something on TV?" he asked.

"If you like. You choose. I'll only half watch anyway."

He scrolled through Netflix on his phone and tapped the icon of a true crime series.

"Ugh, no, not that," My stomach lurched.

The thought of the horrible things people do to each other would only keep me up, worrying about the sort of monsters my children might come across.

He navigated back to the menu and moved on to a show about zombies.

I felt my gorge rise, "Blech, really?"

He sighed, "What then? You said you weren't even going to watch."

"I don't know. What about a car show or something?"

He huffed quietly for a few minutes and then the TV blared to life. He turned it down and we sat companionably for a time.

I grew impatient with my crochet, the blanket I was making used very fine yarn and the rows were relatively long, it was going to take ages to make. I finished one row and decided to go to bed.

"I'll see you in bed?" I turned to Michael.

He frowned, "I thought we were going to snuggle?"

"Yeah, but I'll only fall asleep on the couch and then I won't want to go to bed and I'll get a sore neck..."

"You could have just let me watch my own show then," he grumbled quietly.

"Sorry?" I asked, an edge to my voice and my eyebrow raised.

"Nothing," he said, "I'll see you in bed."

I kissed him and went to bed, snuggling myself down in the blankets and closing my eyes.

Despite my exhaustion, sleep wasn't going to come easily.

I thought back on my conversation with Doctor Imra.

It was bound to only be iron deficiency, or some other vitamin imbalance. I was usually too busy to focus on getting in all my necessary vitamins and minerals, eating all my vegies and all that. I also very rarely ate fruit.

I decided to hit up doctor Google.

One of the first websites that popped up when I searched for anxiety was an anxiety and depression resource site. I had heard of the website before and vaguely knew that they provided support for people with depression.

I read their blurb.

"Feeling anxious in certain situations can help us avoid danger, triggering our 'fight or flight' response. It is how we've evolved to keep ourselves safe. Sometimes though, we can become overly worried about perceived threats – bad things that may or may not happen. When your worries are persistent or out of proportion to the reality of the threat, and get in the way of you living your life, you may have an anxiety disorder.

"When we're very anxious, we have intense feelings of worry or distress that are not easy to control. Anxiety can interfere with how we go about our everyday lives, and make it hard to cope with 'normal' challenges."

I kept reading and found another gem of wisdom.

"Anxiety is the most common mental health condition in Australia. Up to one-third of women and one-fifth of men will experience anxiety at some point in their lives.

I thought about the statistics. That is an awful lot of people to have an anxiety disorder. I wonder if those are only rates of those diagnosed, or if there could be even more.

I hit up Google again to find out more on the statistics. Another website gave me details and quoted the source.

"Australian Bureau of Statistics," I mused, "Seems legit."

I shuddered, the statistics were intimidating.

"One in four people will experience anxiety, fourteen percent of the population will experience an anxiety disorder in a twelve-month period, twelve percent of people will experience PTSD in their lifetime, up to forty percent will experience a panic attack."

93

Oh my god, why don't we learn about this stuff in school. I've never had a panic attack explained to me, but almost half the population will experience one. That's crazy.

I switched over to the statistics on depression.

"Nearly three million Australians live with depression and/or anxiety. Only 35 per cent of Australians with anxiety or depression access treatment. Men are less likely than women to seek treatment, with only 1 in 4 men who experience anxiety or depression seeking treatment. In Australia, it's estimated that 45 per cent of people will experience a mental health condition in their lifetime."

That's crazy. How is there still such a stigma when so many people suffer?

I did a quick Google search on the prevalence of diabetes. Six per cent. Six per cent of people suffer from a form of diabetes and yet almost everyone knows about diabetes and how it can affect people. People don't get judged for having diabetes, even though a large portion of type II diabetes cases could probably be avoided through weight loss and diet changes.

Yet people are judged for having mental health conditions. Almost nine times more people are likely to suffer from a mental health condition than diabetes but more people seem to be willing to accept people despite them having the latter condition than the former.

My eyes had been opened.

But that still didn't mean I had a problem with anxiety.

Chapter Sixteen

*When your eyes are opened to something you should
have been able to see all along.*

"Clare? Can I have a word with you for a minute?"

I had been staring, unseeing, at the Practice finances
for the last five minutes, pondering the safety of the school
play equipment.

The girls should have been outside for their lunchtime
play time and I was half expecting a call saying one of
them had fallen and broken an arm.

*Which one would it be? Amaya tends to knock and
spill things, but Kaylee is a little more accident prone.*

The pointless worrying had taken my attention away
from my computer screen and office and I shook my head
a little as I drew Doctor Imra into focus.

"Yeah, sure," I said.

I tucked my phone into my pocket – in case the school
called – and followed Doctor Imra to her consult room.

"Take a seat," she said, clicking the door behind us.

I sat and watched her cross the room. She was straight
and stiff, this was a professional consult, not a tea room
chat about the weekend.

"I got your blood test results through just now," she
said. She took a deep breath, looked me squarely in the
eyes and said, "Your iron level was right in the middle of
the normal range, I don't think iron deficiency is the cause
of your recent concerns."

"Oh," I said, spiralling into a tailspin of worry, again.

"The good news is, if you do have an anxiety disorder,

it can be treated and you can overcome it."

"I'm fine, though," I said, "Really. If that's what it is, I'll just learn to get over it."

"Clare," there was a note of warning in Doctor Imra's voice, "Mental health conditions aren't something you can just 'get over'. There are tools you can use to help with your symptoms, but they are things that are taught. I need you to go through a few things with me so I can complete the paperwork for you to see a psychologist."

"Fine," I huffed.

"I wrote down your survey scores yesterday, so we don't need to do that again. I don't think it will have changed much in one day."

"Hah," I gave a dry laugh.

Doctor Imra looked at me sharply. I raised an eyebrow at her.

"Clare, is there something you would like to tell me?" She was looking at me like a lioness protecting a cub.

"I may have had a panic attack last night."

She turned her body and attention fully to me and demanded I tell her about it.

"Sounds like a panic attack to me," she turned back to the screen and tapped away at the form.

I played with my fingernails while she worked. They were stained with food colouring from the bath paint I had made the night before. Amaya was going through another bath refusing phase and the only way I could get the wretched child clean was to make paint out of shaving foam and food colouring and withhold it until her face and hair had been washed.

Oh god, how am I going to manage keeping on top of my own condition with all the other stuff I'm trying to keep track of too? I mentally assessed my schedule, trying to find a time slot I could possibly fit in a psychologist appointment.

I thought I had found a spot a week on Tuesday that I might be able to manage it, I would need to arrange to have the afternoon off though and I couldn't possibly go with the children in tow.

"Clare?" Doctor Imra said, from her voice, I don't think it was the first time she'd said my name.

"Hmm?"

"I said, as you know, we have a consultant psychologist here every Friday, I could refer you to her, or we can find another one if you don't want to be seen here for privacy reasons."

"Hah, yeah, that would look good, if everyone thought the practice accountant was going crazy. Everyone would be double-checking their pay, that's for sure."

Doctor Imra gave me a blank stare. "You aren't crazy, Clare, but I will refer you to a psychologist I know. She works in a practice a few minutes down the road, so it won't be too hard for you to get there."

I sighed, "Okay, thank you."

I guess.

"You might not be able to get in for a couple of weeks, so make sure you call for an appointment as soon as you can, I don't want you having to wait too long to get in."

My attention spiked, "Why, what could happen if I have to wait too long?"

She smiled and tried to soothe me, "Nothing in particular will *happen*, but I want you feeling less of those troublesome symptoms, just for your own sake."

I nodded, some of the weight that had settled on my chest lifted. "That makes sense."

"Okay, is there anything else I can do for you today?" Doctor Imra asked me.

"I don't think so," I panicked a little, wondering if there was something I should have asked her.

What if I was meant to ask her something and I didn't and now she thinks I'm crazier than she already does?

The thought spiralled out of control and I mulled over this question for the rest of the afternoon.

"But that's five weeks away," I said, double checking the dates in my calendar.

"Yes," the secretary's voice came through my car

stereo thanks to the Bluetooth connection, "I'm afraid she only works here three days a fortnight, so it can take a while to get in to see her, especially for an initial consult."

I thumped my head down on the steering wheel, my heart was racing at having to wait so long, which didn't even make sense, I only found out that I needed to see someone two hours earlier.

"Okay, I guess that will have to do. Is there a cancellation list you can put me on at all?"

"Of course, I'll pop your name down."

I thanked her and ended the call.

My cheeks felt hot and my palms were clammy. Man, even the appointment worried me.

Is this anxiety? I wondered. *This feeling of being at once squished into the bottom of a can and stretched out like a rubber band, just shy of snapping?*

It was wholly new to me, and very unpleasant.

I remembered Owen's advice of old again, breathing deeply should help.

I left my head resting on the steering wheel of my car and breathed deeply with my eyes closed. It didn't help.

My attention drifted straight to all the jobs I had to do when I got home. Fold the washing, bathe the children, do the readers, cook the dinner, pack the lunches.

My chest got tighter, winding up like the spring in Amaya's racing unicorns.

I heard a car pulling in to the car park and forced myself out of my car. Sitting outside after school care and not collecting my children probably wasn't a good look.

A car door slammed behind me.

"Just getting a few minutes of quiet before unleashing the kraken?" a voice asked behind me.

I turned and saw another mum from Kaylee's class, "Huh?"

She laughed, a little nervously, "I saw you in the car, I thought you might be taking a few minutes of quiet before getting your kids and heading home to the evening chaos. You have two kids, right?"

It took a few seconds for the meaning of her words to

get through the chaos of my worries, "Oh, yeah, right. Yes, I do."

She cocked her head at me, I was being studied. She was counting my legs as if I was one of Amaya's minibeasts. Checking to see if I was an insect or a spider.

"Are you okay? You look a little off."

Can she tell I've been worrying? That I have anxiety?

I rubbed at my forehead, trying to remove the imagined sheen of anxiety from my forehead.

"I'm fine," I said, "Just a headache, it's been a big day."

"I hear you," she said.

She opened the door to the school care and we were barrelled into by our respective children.

We herded our kids to our cars and she beeped her horn and gave me a wave as she drove out of the car park.

Naturally, I was still waiting for my children to get in their car seats.

★   ★   ★

After dinner that night, I decided to message Owen.

He was the only person I knew who'd had anxiety before.

"Hey," I sent when I was curled up on the couch that night, "What's going on?"

I played Sudoku while I waited for a reply; I was too impatient to stare at the little dots.

His reply popped up over my puzzle, "Ahoy! Not much happening here. Just got the mini-me to bed, time for a beer!

"What's happening with you?"

I agonised over the words, trying a few versions, before Owen prompted me to action.

"Spit it out, woman. I can see you typing and deleting, what's going on?" He said.

"I thought I had low iron, because I've been really tired and grumpy lately, but when I spoke to one of the docs at work, my iron was fine and... she thinks I might have anxiety."

I closed the window as soon as the message had sent,

I didn't want to spend the next five minutes agonising over his reply.

"Do you want to talk about it? I can come over."

I looked at Michael, on the two-seater couch opposite me, phone on his chest, head tipped back and snoring gently.

"No need for that."

Still, the offer let a little slack come through on the rubber band that had been pulled tight around my chest all afternoon.

"Okay," he said, "Tell me what's been happening."

I thought about my phrasing for a long time again. "Well, I've been quite tired, as I said before.

"And Trin said the other day that I've been acting a bit funny lately. A little quicker to snap at the kids, and at Michael."

A little fire of shame lit in my chest at the last, Michael was so good to me, it wasn't fair to saddle him with my issues. I decided I wouldn't tell him about the anxiety thing.

As if he was reading my mind, Owen sent, "Have you told Michael yet?"

"No," I hedged, hoping he wouldn't see through to my intentions to leave my husband in the dark. "Anyway, so I guess I have been worrying a bit more than usual, and it's been keeping me awake a little at night and so I've been a bit grumpy."

"Seems legit," Owen said. "How do you feel about that?"

"Well I don't exactly like shouting at my family," I said, "I feel guilty when I growl at them, which I guess just makes it worse. I end up worrying about what sort of emotional scarring I'm giving them."

"Clare, you're their mother, I'm pretty sure 'emotional scarring' is one of the essential parenting expectations. Your kids are great."

"Hah," I said, "In public."

"That's exactly where you want your kids to be great, that way it doesn't look like you're raising complete ferals to your work colleagues.

"Anyway, you're trying to distract me, tell me about your other symptoms. You said you've been worrying, and not sleeping. Any physical symptoms – hot flashes, palpitations, anything like that?"

I had to google 'palpitations' - palpitations are a sensation or awareness of your heart beating.

"Ha, yeah, I guess I have had palpitations lately." I said, "and you know I've always gotten flustered under pressure."

"True that. So, what are you going to about it? Can I help?"

This is why I messaged Owen. No questions, no disbelief, just acceptance and an offer of help.

He was a gem.

"I have an appointment to see a psychiatrist in a few weeks.

"Or was it a psychologist. I can't remember."

He sent me a smiley emoji.

"Here's a handy tip – ology is generally something to do with language or talking, so a psychologist is someone who talks to help you. Psychiatrists talk too, but they have a medical degree and can prescribe medication."

"Ha, the more you know." I said, trying to remember his fun fact along with the last time I brushed the girls' hair.

"Will you be okay?" He asked.

I allowed my emotions to lay themselves out before me. I felt raw, scoured, like I had been scrubbed with steel wool, or cleaned out with a hot vindaloo.

"I think so," I typed.

"Good." He said. "I'm here if you need anything, okay? And tell Michael! Love you xox"

I sighed and put my phone down, then picked it up again, remembering my Sudoku.

How could I possibly feel so awful when I had so much good in my life?

Chapter Seventeen

One day I'm going to find the police on my doorstep and will have to explain that the screams were just the result of my trying to brush my daughter's wobbly tooth.

Mornings always seem to follow the same pattern.

Get up, get ready, pack the bags. Wake the kids, feed the kids, scream at the kids to 'put on your school uniforms, we do this every day, why are you acting like it's such a surprise, it's part of our normal routine'.

I was going to go back to making them wear school clothes to bed every night instead of just when they had to go to OSHC in the morning.

Then there was always an issue with shoes. I don't know why they could never find their shoes. If by some chance I manage to find a pair, it is never the pair they want, and the ones they want are separated. By the time you find the pair they want, they have changed their minds again.

And that's before we've even managed to get out of the house.

Through some miracle, I occasionally manage to get to work on time.

There was a lot of work to catch up on; I had been less than productive after talking to Doctor Imra the previous afternoon. After ploughing through most of the backlog I was surprised that I had made it to midday without a break.

Naturally, my stomach growled as soon as I noticed the time.

I retrieved my lunch and eyeballed my salad of rather droopy lettuce and overripe tomato. I picked out the cubes of cheese and decided to supplement it with a cup of soup.

I had completely forgotten about the anxiety thing until I saw a message pop up from Owen.

"How you doing, sunshine?" A winky face emoji partnered his message.

"I'm fine." I replied. "How are you?"

I wondered why he was messaging me; we didn't usually talk in the work day unless one of us needed advice.

The memory of our conversation from the night returned with a solid whack to my stomach.

Why did I tell him that? It's probably nothing. It will just make him worry. He doesn't need to worry about me, worry distracts people. What if he worries about me on his drive home and forgets to pick Alfie up from childcare. Today is his turn for collection.

The ding of my phone interrupted my worrying.

"Good. I'm good." Owen said. "Hey, I was thinking."

Great. He is worrying and thinking about me. I bet he hasn't been focussing at work today either, he'll probably get fired because of me.

"Don't worry about me," I typed before he could get fired, "I'll be fine, you just get back to work. I don't want you to get in trouble."

"Clare, I'm not going to get in trouble at work because I'm looking out for you. You helped me out back in the day, now it's my turn to help you."

I smiled and felt tears prick my eyes, "Thanks."

"Now, I was thinking, sometimes mental health disorders can be worsened when you aren't able to express yourself properly."

"Does that mean I should swear more? That would help me express myself."

"Funny," he said, "But you're deflecting with humour.

"I mean, are you still suppressing and ignoring certain... skills that you possess."

A string of emoji followed his statement: a trio of

stars, a magic eight-ball, a crystal ball.

My arms grew cold and I glanced around to make sure no-one could see my messages over my shoulder.

"You said you'd never talk about that Owen." I typed furiously.

"We're not talking, are we?" The bastard sent me the tongue out emoji.

"Nomenclature."

"Anyway, I always disagreed with your decision not to use your magic once you had Kaylee. I can only imagine that it would be a massive help around the house."

I sighed, "It's not like that and you know it."

And he did know it too.

Before I met Michael, Owen and I had spent a lot of time together. We had been together on group projects, read each other's essays and crammed together at exam times.

During a particularly gruelling cram session I had forgotten myself and got a fresh can of drink from the fridge – by levitating it to the table.

Owen had been understandably freaked out, but calmed down once I showed him a few tricks.

Although he also never understood why I hadn't found any spells to improve my memory at those critical points in our undergraduate studies.

"How many witches are there in the world, Clare? How many of them do you think impose stupid rules on themselves like you do?"

"I told you not to use the 'w' word." I said, "I prefer the term 'magically abled'. It's non-gender specific."

"Fine. Magically abled." I imagine the sarcasm dripping from his tone as if he had spoken the words instead of typed.

A door opened behind me and jolted me out of the conversation. I bumped my knee on my desk and held in a swear word as I turned around to address a question put to me.

A veritable essay waited for me when I turned back to my phone.

"And I don't know why you never told Michael about the magic either. I know, I know, your Mum told you stories about couples who had broken up over the magic. Partners who would never quite believe that their magically abled other half had really never used any magic against them, but I just don't think Michael would be like that.

"Your home life could be so much easier if you just used a little magic in your life."

"Owen! You know it isn't as simple as that. You saw all the crap I had to do to be able to practice. By the time I've collected my crystals and grown all my herbs and all the other stuff, I may as well have just vacuumed the carpet manually."

"Yeah, I guess," he said. "I just wanted to help."

I don't need help. I resolutely told myself.

For politeness I replied, "I know, thank you. I appreciate it. Catch up on the weekend?"

"Defs," he sent me a smiley.

I responded in kind and set my phone down.

"Oh man," I said aloud, placing my face in my hands.

What have I unleashed?

I thought he was back to prod me when the phone dinged again that afternoon, but it was Trin.

I had finally managed to make it through some of my work, so I decided I could take a ten minute coffee break to chat.

Her message was cryptic. "Hey lady, are you wrinkly?"

I turned the question over, but couldn't make sense of it.

"What have you been taking today?" I asked.

"Well, it's either that or you are iron-y. Get it, your iron levels? Low iron means wrinkly."

I tossed up how to respond, in the end I gave her both insults, "If you have to explain the joke, it probably wasn't that funny. And you and your husband deserve each other for sense of dad humour alone."

She sent me a poking out tongue emoji.

"Anyway," she sent, "Have you had your iron levels checked yet?"

"As a matter of fact I have," *because I knew that if I didn't you would keep pestering me until I did.*

"And? What was the verdict? Was Trin right again?"

I smiled, only crazy people referred to themselves in the third person.

"Sadly, this will not be chalked up as a win for Trin.

"My iron levels are perfectly fine."

"Ha!" she said, "That is strange, it's really rare for me to be wrong."

A guilty tinge of heartburn rose behind my sternum.

"You can't win 'em all." I sent her a winky face. "Thanks for checking on me though."

"Anytime xo."

I returned the kiss and hug and felt like a terrible friend for not telling her that she was partly right. There was something wrong with me, it just wasn't my iron.

Somehow, my mother found out.

She had probably been scrying me again.

"Clarissa?" I knew she knew from the moment she waltzed herself through my front door.

"In the kitchen," I braced myself for a lecture.

I glanced out of the kitchen window to check out on the girls. Their voices drifted through the screen. It sounded like one of their regular games of café was well in play.

"Clare? Come here."

I held myself stiff as I succumbed to my mother's embrace. The scent of lavender and rosemary engulfed me. She had probably dabbed on the essential oils just before coming over so I could benefit from their soothing effects.

Yes, I still remembered all about my essential oils.

"Sit down, sit down," she said, ordering me around in my own kitchen, "I'll make you a cup of tea."

She put the kettle on and bustled around my kitchen, pulling ingredients out of thin air.

Literally.

I was also fairly certain that I had never owned a proper teapot, but apparently I did now. It was quite a nice one, too.

She muttered under her breath and reached an empty hand into the air, then pulled it down and placed a handful of herbs into the teapot. She repeated the process several times. Only when she leaned on the dining table and stretched out awkwardly did I realise she was using a transposition spell to grab ingredients from her own kitchen.

"Show off," I said, the words sour in my mouth, "You know you could have just brought all those things over from your house instead of procuring them from here."

"No, I couldn't. I wasn't home when I was..." she trailed off, stopping her movements as if hoping I wouldn't register the meaning of her words.

"When you were what, Mother?"

She was looking out the kitchen window and I thought I saw a hint of red on the top of her ears, "Oh look..."

I cut her off, "Don't try to use my own children to distract me. When you were what?"

If I'd been practicing I would have woven a pull of compulsion to my voice. As it was, I had to settle with my mum tone.

"Nothing," she said, "I just thought it was high time I dropped by."

"Mum."

"I was out and I thought I would visit my lovely daughter and granddaughters. I don't know why you are treating me like I have criminal motives."

"I feel thou doth protest too much."

I drew a little magic from the kitchen. Creating something, even a simple bolognaise sauce, also creates a little magic residue which can be utilised.

I enhanced my sense of smell and studied Mum's aura.

"Mrs Corney!" I said. I snapped my fingers and turned the window glass into a mirror, reflecting my mother's sheepish face, "You've been scrying with Mrs Corney again, haven't you? Honestly Mum, I thought you'd stopped that. I told you, I'm a grown adult now, I can take care of myself!"

"Clare!" I could feel the tug of her voice on me.

"Don't you use magic on me!"

The pull eased.

"Fine, I'm sorry I tried. It's not that we're spying. We just miss our kids. You were my entire world and focus for so long that it's been hard for me to let go."

"I moved out when I got married, Mum."

"I know!"

"Ten years ago!"

"I know! I just miss you is all."

I sighed.

"Alright, I know. Although I can't imagine doing anything but dance for joy at the idea of my house staying clean for longer than five minutes after they grow up and move out - I get it."

The lines of tension eased from her face. She smiled. "Thanks."

"So, what did you see in your spying?"

"Scrying," she corrected. "I saw your unprotected aura. It was an absolute mess, Clare. What's going on?"

I sighed, "I spoke to one of the doctors at work yesterday. She thinks I might have anxiety."

"Oh, Clare." She moved toward me, but glanced back at her reflection in the mirror-window. "Did you sound proof that as well?"

I knitted my unkempt eyebrows, "No? Oh."

The sound of little voices no longer wafted through the window pane.

The dreaded sound of silence.

Oh god, what are they up to now?

A barrage of images assaulted me.

Injuries would end in screaming, so clearly they weren't harmed. Unless they were unconscious. Could they have both have knocked each other out? Could they have been kidnapped from our own backyard? The side gate didn't have a lock and I hadn't been watching them. How would I explain that to Michael?

He would never forgive me.

I would never forgive myself.

"Whoa, Clare!" Mum said, "What is going on with you?"

Her eyes took on a silvery hue and I knew she was studying my aura as I sank to the ground and pressed myself against the kitchen cupboards. I closed my eyes. I felt my heart thumping in my chest. A band constricted tight around my ribs. Air eked into my lungs.

The images kept blurring through my mind, a terrible slideshow of things that could have happened to my children.

"Clare? Drink this," a mug was pressed into my hands.

Steam caressed my face.

Peppermint and lemon balm teased my nose.

A gentle touch of honey rolled on my tongue when I sipped.

I breathed in the gentle aroma deeply.

Five things to see, four things to feel, three things to hear, two things to smell, one thing to taste.

I opened my eyes.

See – Kaylee at the table, Amaya next to her, Mum sitting with them, the unfamiliar teapot, the chipping lacquer on my fingernails.

Feel – my numb bum on the floor, the doorknob behind my head, the hole in my sock, the scalding heat of the tea in the mug.

Hear – the kids talking, the drip of the tap, the birds outside

Smell – the tea, the musty cupboards

Taste – the tea.

The tea.

I breathed out deeply and finished the tea.

I could no longer feel the thumping of my heart when the mug was empty. I felt like my body had enough oxygen. My bum was still numb.

I stood up slowly, my legs felt shaky.

I washed my mug and caught Mum staring at me in the still mirrored window.

I pulled a little more magic from the kitchen walls and fixed the window. Mum's reflection became a watermark over the view of the backyard.

"Have you finished your snacks now, girls?" Mum asked.

"Yep," said Kaylee.

"Mmhmm," agreed Amaya.

"Okay, back outside you go then."

"Not for long though, okay?" I said, "It will be bath time soon."

I'd find energy for that effort somewhere. I had to.

"Okay Mama," Amaya said. She walked up beside me and squeezed my leg. "I love you."

I ruffled her hair, "I love you too, baby."

The shouting started before the door had even slammed closed behind them.

I smiled at Kaylee's retreating calls, "Amaya, let's play on the trampoline!"

"They're good kids," Mum came to stand next to me, watching them out the window.

I snorted, "Yeah, provided you don't let them play hairdresser with a real pair of scissors."

"Really, though, that probably was partly your own fault, why did they even have the scissors?"

"What?" I glowered at my mother, "What do you mean? It's not like they're babies anymore, we should be able to trust them with scissors. It's not like when Amaya trimmed your cat's whiskers when she was three. She knows better now.

"Besides which," my voice was now rising, "I had only gotten home a few minutes before they cut my hair, so even if they shouldn't have had the scissors, the fault in supervision was Michael's, not mine!"

A shattering crash jolted my eyes away from Mum's face.

The water in the glasses on the table was still shivering and the shards of my favourite mug glittered menacingly on the floor.

I studied the sharp edges in stunned silence.

"Was there an earthquake?" I asked.

"No, Clare. There was a witch quake."

Chapter Eighteen

Did you ever feel like you could skewer someone with a stare? Some days I have to be careful to not do just that.

"This is why you need my help." Mum ushered me to the dining table and pulled out a chair.

She waved a hand and my mug was once again whole and on the table in front of me. The effortless use of magic sickened me.

"It is not effortless and you know it!" Mum said, "I put a lot of time and work into building up my stores of magic."

"Get out of my head," I said, "It's crowded enough in there already, I don't need another person in there too."

"I can see that." Mum said, tartly, "And I'm not trying to get in, you just haven't got any recognisable layer of shield up at the moment, you must have shredded it with that break out."

I ran my thumb over my fingernails as she spoke: index, central, ring, pinkie.

"What do I do, Mum?" I paused my fidgeting and searched her eyes. "Having kids is meant to be the best and most rewarding thing someone ever does. At the moment it just seems like they're holding the key to my cell of drudgery and toil."

"Having kids is hard work."

"Why didn't anyone tell me that before I had two of the suckers? Everyone thought I was mad when I fell pregnant again before Kaylee's first birthday, but no-one ever told me that they were likely to take me to the brink of sanity and then push me over. No-one busted out the cautionary tales until after it was already too late."

"Oh, Clare..."

"No, don't you try to commiserate, you didn't say anything either. There are so many damn taboos in this society that stories that should be told as warnings end up being told to sympathise instead. It's bullshit."

I was pacing now.

"Do I need to get you a Valium?"

"I don't even know what that is! Anyway, I don't have any time to wallow in self-pity; I need to get shit done."

I bashed about with pots and pans, setting up to cook dinner and pack the lunchboxes and unstack the dishwasher – for the fifty thousandth night in a row.

"Would you like me to take the kids to the bath for you?"

"Yes, please. That would be great." My temper hadn't receded, I was still growling.

Mum knew me well enough to ignore my tone.

I snort-laughed.

It wasn't quite the full belly-laugh that the meme deserved, but it was all I could manage.

Michael looked up at me from the other end of the couch.

"What?" he asked.

"Nosey!" I said, "Nothing you need to concern yourself with."

The picture was part of a long-running joke stream I was sharing with Owen. It would have taken too long to explain it to Michael and it wouldn't have been funny by the time I reached the end.

"Fine," he sniffed, "Then I won't tell you the water cooler gossip today."

"Oooh, was it about Michelle in HR's latest hook up? Is she still working her way through the marketing department?"

The salacious gossip always fuelled a certain cattiness of my spirit.

"Nope, I'm not telling you," he said.

I smiled, assuming he was winding me up, "Come on! You know there's no gossip in my office, hook me up, this stuff is my life blood."

"Then you should watch The Bachelor, there's plenty of it on there."

I slumped back, "You're really not going to tell me?"

He raised his brows and kept his focus on his phone.

Irritatingly, tears pricked my eyes. *What a prat.*

I stayed on the couch for a minute, squeezing my eyes fiercely. When I thought I could keep my voice steady, I stood.

"Good night," I said, in the coldest voice I could muster.

"Where are you going?" he asked.

"To bed."

"What? Why?"

"Because I'm tired." I was already in the doorway, facing out.

I stood for a moment, waiting – hoping - for him to call me back. But he didn't.

"Fine," he said.

His voice was cold. I shivered.

I cried myself to sleep.

"Hey, Clare, how are you?"

Doctor Imra came in to the staff kitchen-come-breakroom to grab her lunch just as I was finishing mine.

My mind is a wreck, my magic is leaking, I'm not entirely sure why I had kids and I think my marriage is falling apart.

"Peachy."

"Good to hear."

Sometimes my verbal irony is just lost on people.

"Did you manage to get in to see that lady I referred you to?"

I glanced around, she hadn't been specific, but I still wanted to make sure no-one had heard.

"No," I finally answered, "She's fully booked for the

next five weeks."

"And how have your symptoms been?"

She noticed me look around again.

"I was going to eat in my office, would you like to join me?"

I sighed, recognising it as an instruction, not a request. "Sure, why not."

I cradled a hot cup of tea in my hands and followed Doctor Imra to her office.

"Do you have anything you'd like to tell me?" She asked when we were settled as Doctor and Patient again.

Last night I lost control of my magic and created a localised Clare-quake in my kitchen. I smashed my favourite mug, but it's alright because Mum was there and she fixed it right up for me. I'm sure you'll want to know if she used a food safe glue on the ceramic, but there's no need to worry, she used her magic on it instead.

"I had another panic attack last night."

"Okay, do you know what the trigger was?"

"Trigger?"

"The trigger. There is usually a thought or a concern that starts a panic attack. It's called a trigger."

"Huh," *you learn something new every day.* "I had been talking to my mum, having a bit of a disagreement really. Then we noticed that the kids were quiet. It's not like them to be quiet. It usually just means they are getting into mischief, but I thought that something might have happened to them..."

"You got caught up in worrying about them?"

I nodded. Saying what I had imagined was too hard. I couldn't bring myself to vocalise the hideous thoughts.

"That is a symptom of your anxiety, Clare. I'm worried about you. I think that your symptoms will worsen as you worry about your anxiety as well. I'm going to give the practice a call and see what I can do for you, okay?"

I felt as though I should be grateful for her intervention, but I also partly blamed her for saying the word 'anxiety' in the first place.

115

As though if she hadn't labelled me, I wouldn't be suffering at all.

Chapter Nineteen

I really must start writing down my one-liners as I think of them.

"Hi, is that Clarissa Willoughby?" A female voice asked.

I wedged the phone up to my ear with my shoulder and went back to chopping the salad vegetables for dinner.

"That's me."

"Hi Clarissa, I'm calling from Whole Health, we had you booked for an appointment with Rachel Chiante in a few weeks?"

"Yep, I think it was the 28th?"

"That's right. I'm just calling as we've had a cancellation for this Thursday afternoon at 4pm, I was wondering if you'd like to take that appointment?"

I did a mental shuffle. I wouldn't need to finish work early, the kids might have to stay at OSHC a little late, but I could make that work.

"Yeah, thanks, that would be great."

I pulled the phone away from my ear and put the woman on speaker so I could update the appointment details in my phone calendar.

"Okay, so that's all booked in for you, this Thursday at 4pm."

"Thanks very much," I hung up and put the phone down next to the chopping board.

Well, that should be good. I might be able to get over this anxiety stuff faster and get back to my normal life. I wonder how cancellations come up with psychologists?

Do people just get better? Or maybe it's because someone got worse. I don't want to take an appointment from someone who is suffering worse than me... no, that wouldn't happen. It's probably just that someone had to work unexpectedly. Yeah, that's it.

I had palpitations again. I refused to do the senses check, it wasn't that bad. I shook my head and got back to cooking.

But really though, what could have happened to free up an appointment? Do they get notified if one of their patients falls victim to their illness?

I put the knife down, placed my hands flat on the bench on either side of the chopping board, closed my eyes and breathed deeply.

What is wrong with me? Why am I focussing on that sort of rubbish when I should just be getting on with cooking dinner?

I growled at myself and finished chopping my potatoes and onions.

That job done, I picked up my tray and headed out the back.

The barbecue had seen better days, but it still cooked amazing potato chips.

I tried to block out the anxious thoughts while I lit the gas and scraped the grill.

What if she says I'm not fit to be a parent?

The thought had my chest tightening again, a burning feeling bubbling up behind my sternum.

I couldn't focus on the plate as I followed the motions of cooking the dinner. Oil on the plate, potatoes on top, onions at the back, chops on the grill.

My breathing got heavier, the rubber band around my chest turned to steel, cold and tight, my vision swam. I tried to blame the shimmering over the hot plate on heat haze, but it knew it wasn't the case.

I dropped the tongs when I felt a weight land on my shoulder.

Eight little pin pricks dug into my shoulder, four in front of my collarbone, four on my back. A warm weight settled on my shoulder. A quiet chittering sounded in my ear. A softness brushed against my neck. My earlobe was pinched.

"Ouch!"

I nearly dislodged the bird perched on my shoulder when I flung my hand up to my injured earlobe.

"What was that for?" I screeched, competing with the bird for volume and pitch.

"That?" the galah said, "That was just a love peck."

"Crikey! I'd hate to feel what you could do with that beak in anger!"

I pulled my hand away from my earlobe and held it flat in front of my shoulder. The weight transferred from my shoulder to my hand.

I pulled my hand forward and studied the bird.

"Eneya, to what do I owe the pleasure?"

"Saw Clare while flying."

The bird wouldn't look me in the eye. A lot of birds, particularly the larger ones, are keenly intelligent and can recognise faces; and read auras.

"Really? Just flying over? Did my mother happen to ask you to fly over?"

Eneya ground her beak and kept avoiding my eye.

I brought her little body up to my chest and kissed her head.

"Thank you."

She pressed her head against my chin and I breathed in the scent of her; dusty earth, eucalyptus and the special scent that was unique to feathers.

I dragged an outdoor chair next to the barbecue and set Eneya on the back of it. She started preening.

I grabbed the tongs off the ground, wiped them on my apron and started turning my potato slices over.

"How are your hatchlings?" I asked.

"Growing," she sounded pleased and proud, "Feathers coming in. In several more sunrises, feathers of flight will be tested."

"That must be a stressful time for you."

"What stress?" the bird paused her preening, wing

outstretched, to study me.

"You know, when you worry about something so much that your heart beats faster."

"Worry?" the little bird cocked her head in avian puzzlement.

"Thinking about all the things that can go wrong?" I tried to put it in terms a bird would understand, "Like thinking there might be a cat outside the nest when your babies pop their heads out."

"Clever cat to rise so high. Our nest many branches above ground, no easy branches for cats to climb."

I had to wrap my head around that. Birds use the term 'branch' in both the human sense and as a unit of measurement.

I sighed, "What if a cat approaches you - nears you - when you are on the grass eating? Or a human walks too near?"

"I fly away."

Perhaps this concept is a little too big for a bird.

I gave it one last try.

"What do you feel right before you fly? If a cat is going to pounce?"

"Thundering breast, twitching toes, stretching wings."

"Yes! That is stress."

The bird twittered unintelligibly – at least to my ears.

"When humans stress, do they empty?"

I turned the word over, but couldn't figure it. I asked Eneya.

"Empty."

Failing to find the words to explain, the bird pooped. A smear of white streaked down the back of the chair and onto the deck.

I rolled my eyes, "Thank you for that eloquent explanation."

"You're welcome," she said.

Apparently birds were immune to my verbal irony too.

I plucked the meat and potatoes off the barbecue and started to scrape the grill and plate clean.

"Your others approach," trilled Eneya, "Safe flights."

I glanced up from my work to watch the bird rise with a 'cheech, cheech' call.

A spike of envy hit me. The bird didn't even know what stress was. She cared for her hatchlings for a little over twelve weeks and then went back to looking out for herself and Dash.

I sighed.

The side gate bashed open and Kaylee and Amaya came running through, shouting for me. Michael followed close behind, looking a little sheepish.

I narrowed my eyes at him and knelt down to receive jubilant hugs from the girls.

"Mama, Mama, guess what!" Amaya said.

"What?"

"Daddy took us to the shops and we got..." Kaylee said.

"No," shrieked Amaya, "I want to tell her."

Wow, I think that was a record, they were home for at least thirty seconds before the screaming started.

"Fine." Amaya said.

"What did you get, Kaylee?"

Her face split into a grin again, "We got a kitty!"

"You got a what?" I asked.

"A kitty cat!" Kaylee repeated.

My fingers went from normal to peak magic tingle in 0.01 seconds.

I turned a blank face to Michael.

He shrugged, "The shelter had a stand set up in the shopping centre for an adoption day thing. The girls have wanted a pet for a while and you said they might be able to have a cat one day..."

'One day' in the way that means 'never' but I don't want to say 'no' outright because I don't want to pointlessly argue with them.

"Oh, that's great."

Michael was well trained in detecting my verbal irony.

A swift look of 'oh shit' passed across his features.

"I know, I know, I should have told you about it first,

or asked you, rather, it's just, you've seemed so stressed lately and they say that having pets can reduce your stress levels..."

Maybe when you aren't the one who has to pick up after it.

"I thought it might help," he finished.

The girls started nattering excitedly at me about the selection process and all the things they'd bought for the little beast.

My heart sank, we were stuck with it.

"Alright, alright, you'd best go in and wash your hands for dinner and we'll put the kitty somewhere quiet to settle in before we start playing." I turned to Michael, "I'm guessing it's in a carrier?"

"Yep," he smiled proudly, "The stand was right outside the cheap shop, I went in and grabbed one before the girls chose."

"Still in the car?"

He nodded.

"You'd best put it in the lounge with all its gear then. I'll set the table and we'll try to get the kids to eat before we let it out. They'll be hopeless otherwise."

He drew me in for a hug and I reluctantly kissed him.

"Is that okay? I thought you might like a pet, something fluffy to cuddle."

"Thank you, it was a wonderful thought."

He read between the lines.

"But not a wonderful action?"

"We'll see. I'll try to reserve judgement."

He grinned at me and planted a proper kiss on my lips.

"You're going to love him."

"Him? Are you sure you didn't get the cat just to even the gender odds a little?"

"Maybe!" He disappeared around the side of house.

I closed the lid on the barbecue and took the tray of food inside.

Honestly, I let them go to the shops without me once and they buy a cat! I thought women were meant to be the impulse buyers.

I would have thought that at some point in the last twelve years that Michael might have gotten the point about me not really being a pet person. It's not that I don't like animals, I had always loved it when Dash and Eneya came to visit, it was just that people looked at you strangely when you talked to animals.

I mean, everyone talks to animals, but people seem to notice when you start listening for their responses...

Life was about to get even more complicated.

Chapter Twenty

I love animals and, in general, they like me, it just gets a little awkward when people think you are actually talking to their dog.

"Ok, girls, you need to calm down, or you'll scare the poor little thing."

Kaylee and Amaya were giggling excitedly as they tried to catch a peek of the twelve week old kitten hiding under a hand towel in the carry case.

As usual, thirty seconds later they were whinging because they were in each other's way and neither could see in.

"Hands on top," I said.

"That means stop," the girls finished the phrase, sat back and put their hands on their heads.

That phrase seriously worked better than any magic I could consider using on them.

"Right, you two, back away from the carry case."

"But we want to see!" Amaya whined.

"I know," I said, "You two are very excited, but you need to think about the kitty for a minute. He is in a new place, he's probably had a scary ride in the car and there's all this noise! He's only a baby; you need to let him come out in his own time."

The girls shot me mutinous looks.

"So," I said, "This is what we will do. While Daddy is setting up the litter tray and food bowls in the laundry, we'll sit in here with the door to the kitty cage open and let him come out in his own time. I'll put the TV on for you, would you like to choose a movie?"

The squabble over the movie selection ('I want to choose.' 'No, she got to choose last time.' 'No I didn't!') lasted a full five minutes. They then wanted to sit on the floor to watch the kitten, so I arranged cushions for them to sit on, which they then moved closer to the carry case.

I left the kids where they were and moved the kitten.

Finally, with the opening credits of the movie playing, I opened the door to the carrier and took a peek.

"Hey, baby." I said.

I was met with silence from the kitten and outrage from the children.

"Mama, you said we had to let the kitten out on its own."

I sighed. *Why are they so good at pointing out when I don't do what I've told them to?*

I didn't answer the impertinent child, but I did move away from the carrier.

I sat with my back resting against the couch, wineglass in one hand and Sudoku in the other. I hummed a cat lullaby I had learned in my youth, just loud enough so the little kitten could hear me.

"Many little whiskers,
Four little paws,
Two little ears,
Twenty little claws.
Come now little one,
Cuddle near,
Share the warm fur,
Mama is here."

A little mew answered my song and two little heads turned away from the TV.

"Mama, the kitten meowed. Can we get him out?" Amaya asked.

Shopkins. I felt the kitten withdraw again at Amaya's excited voice.

"What did I say? Leave him be."

They reluctantly turned back to their movie. I went back to my humming and puzzles.

Michael lumbered in just as I sensed the kitten was getting curious.

"Where is it?" I swear his voice at that moment would have shaken windows.

"Shhh." I glowered at him. "It's still in the box."

"Why haven't you gotten it out?"

"We're letting him out on his own terms."

I had to wait a minute before I could start humming again. I was now getting impatient. I didn't know what the little guy looked like and I wanted to see him.

Everyone settled back again and I kept humming.

"Clare?" Michael had sat on the couch with his knees at my shoulder.

I looked up to meet his puzzled eyes.

"Are you *purring*?"

I had forgotten that the lullaby was sung in the key of purr. It had only been in the house for an hour and I had already made my first slip up. Great.

At least I hadn't been miaowing.

"What? Why would I be purring? I've been humming to myself."

"Humming?"

"Yes, humming." The defensive tone was necessary, I very rarely hummed. Sang – yes. Whistled- definitely. Hummed – not so much.

"Okay."

He looked at me as though I had sprouted ears and a tail of my own. Never mind that I could actually do that if I needed to, he didn't need to know that.

After another fifteen minutes of humming (purring) I noticed a little head peering out of the cat carrier.

The kitten was at the lanky stage. Long legs, big head and a skinny little tail.

He took a few steps out of the cage, revealing a mostly snowy white, short haired coat. The tips of his ears, his paws, tail and nose were all black.

He was not the sort of cat to be immediately identified as a witch's familiar.

He walked slowly and carefully toward me, glancing

around the room as he went. I kept humming.

He moved the length of my legs and raised a tentative paw to my lap. I lifted a hand and scritched behind his ear. He purred and climbed into my lap.

I relaxed as his little body curled up, my hand in his fur, and fell asleep.

I took a photo of the little furball and sent it to Trin.

"I let them go to the shops without me again."

"OH. MY. GOD." Trin said, "Is that real?"

"Well, it isn't a taxidermy."

"Seriously? They went to the shops, for what, milk? And came home with a kitten?"

"Pretty much. I thought women were the only ones who did that."

"I thought you weren't a pet person?" She asked.

"I'm not, really. I'm not entirely sure what possessed him to buy a kitten. Probably pester-power from the kids." I tacked an eye-roll emoji onto the end of my text.

"So, is he going to last the night?"

"Michael or the kitten?" I asked.

"Either."

"Well, apparently they are both house trained and I don't think the kids would be worth living with if I turfed either of them out. And unhappy kids aren't worth living with."

"Ain't that the truth." Trin typed. "At least the snuggles look nice."

"Yeah, he's pretty cute."

I rubbed behind one of his ears and he gave a 'prrt' of pleasure.

Okay, I probably could say I was happy with the addition.

I was not as pleased with him when he jumped on my face at 5AM the next morning.

I instinctively hissed my displeasure. My cheeks reddened when I remembered Michael was snuggling into my back.

"Sorry!" he grunted, "I'll go lock him in the laundry."

"No. If you do that, he'll just cry. He's had his breakfast and is ready to play."

"Mmmph."

The little kitten climbed onto my pillow and burrowed into my hair.

"I hope you're too little to have fleas." I said.

"What are fleas?" The little kitten asked.

"Tiny biters. You'll work it out if you ever get them."

He snuggled down in the nape of my neck, purring, and went back to sleep.

Naturally, having been woken, I was now wide awake and thinking about the argument I still needed to have with Michael.

I couldn't believe he had bought the cat without telling me. Okay, so it seemed well behaved and was litter trained and hadn't cried all through the night, but that was beside the point.

I built up a big enough head of steam that I delivered quite a sharp elbow to his ribs when he snored loud enough to wake the kitten.

"What?" He rose to a half sitting position.

"You were snoring."

"Oh, sorry. Well, don't you look comfortable there."

I sensed more than felt him reach out to scratch the kitten.

"I'm glad *he's* happy." I said

Michael stopped moving.

"What's wrong, Clare?" he sounded exasperated.

So was I.

"Just that you brought more responsibility home for me without actually talking to me about it first."

"I bought him for you!" he said.

"Yes, I know, and I appreciate that you were thinking about me and trying to help, but really, it's just something else for me to look after. Another job on my to-do-list!" I was whisper-shouting, "Do you even know how much I have to do on any given day?"

"Then let me do some of it!" His whisper shout was husky and I would have found it hot if it wasn't for all the other stuff going on between us.

"When will you have time? You work more than I do!"

The kitten sensed the tension and wisely legged it. I rolled over to face Michael.

"I just don't think you realise how much I have to do to keep this house functional. It's not easy."

Despite all my efforts, I burst into tears.

"Oh, Clare," he said, "Come here."

He lay on his back and pulled me into his chest, holding me tight while I sobbed.

I wiped my face on the quilt cover when I succeeded in supressing the tears. I heaved a sigh and pulled my head up to rest in the nook of his shoulder.

"Hey," he said. He shifted so he could look at me. "What's going on with you lately?"

This was, if I had wanted it, the best opportunity I had to tell him about my anxiety, but I couldn't. It felt like I was confessing a sin. That I couldn't handle taking care of my family and managing the finances and the washing and the food and all the other jobs.

That if I couldn't take care of him and our daughters, he would want to find someone else who could.

"I don't know," I said, "I guess I'm just getting used to the scramble and I was a little hurt that you didn't discuss the cat with me first."

"I'm sorry." He said, sincerity in his tone as he studied me, "I didn't realise it would be such a big thing for you. I'll take it back."

I shook my head. "Are you kidding, the girls will never speak to you again. It will be fine, but you can do the food and the toilet. I'll just take the cuddles."

He smiled and grabbed my hand. He twined our fingers together and I smiled back.

"Deal."

I snuggled back down on his chest and listened to his heartbeat.

"It's very early," he said. His hand wandered down my back and snapped the elastic on my underwear. "The children probably won't wake up for at least an hour."

Man, am I totally disinterested. How can I best get out of this?

"Unless we start doing what you are implying, in which case they'll be up right at a critical moment."

His hand roamed far enough to cup my butt.

"Honey," I gently pushed as he moved to kiss me with intent.

"Hmm," his breath was hot on my neck.

"I'm sorry, I'm just... I'm really not that interested right now."

He let go of my hand and flopped back.

"Fine," he said, "I guess I'll just get up and have a shower then."

He gave me a peck, and then tried it on once more, poking his tongue in my mouth.

I laughed and pushed him off properly, "Go away."

"Fine."

As he walked from the room I mused that he would be very clean for work – he would probably have a *very* long shower.

Chapter Twenty One

All the love songs and stories are about falling in love,
none of them ever seem to tell you how to stay in love.

The kitten wove between my legs as I walked, doing its very best to trip me up.

"Achh," I hissed.

The kitten scuttled away and I made it the rest of the way to the lounge room without spilling either of the coffees.

"Here," I said.

"Thank you. Oh the sweet elixir of life!" Owen said.

I shook my head, "You worry me."

"What doesn't worry you right now, Clare?"

A jolt went through me. "That's not kind."

"No, I meant it seriously. What doesn't worry you?"

I couldn't give him an honest answer.

When I walked down the street with the girls I worried about someone losing control of their car. When I cooked dinner I worried about one of them being hurt or that I would discover one of them had a food allergy when I inadvertently gave them an anaphylactic reaction to something new. I worried about Michael when I knew he was driving home from work – sometimes I even watched his little icon on Google maps, checking it every few minutes until he arrived home. I even worried about the little kitten now, that his natural curiosity would lead him to trouble.

The kitten himself jumped up onto the couch next to me and purred.

"No need to worry for me, people mama." He said, laying the length of his body along my thigh.

I rubbed his tummy.

"You even worry about him don't you?" Owen pointed.

"Maybe," I said, avoiding Owen's eye.

"And that, Clare, is why you need help."

Owen moved to sit on the sofa with me.

"Some worry is perfectly fine and normal, but if you can't enjoy little bits of everyday life, it's a sign that your worry has gotten the better of you. It's time to get some help to deal with it," he said. "You have told Michael haven't you?"

"Michael doesn't need to know." I answered quickly.

"Clare, he lives with you. He's your husband. He should know."

I squirmed, "I don't want him to know."

Owen sighed. "Why not?"

"Because I feel like a failure! I feel like I should be able to do everything and be everything to everyone, without completely falling apart."

"Well there's your problem!" Owen said. "No-one can be everything to everyone. Sometimes you just need to be you, for yourself."

I glared at him.

"Okay. Obviously, that is not a lesson you can hear from me. You've got an appointment to see a psychologist?"

"Yeah, on Thursday after work."

"Okay. Let's talk about something else then. How about that local sporting team?"

I gave him a flat stare, "Owen, neither of us follow sport. Let's go see what the kids are up to."

We carried our coffee mugs out to the back yard. Kaylee was pushing Owen's son, Alfie, on the swing and Amaya was pulling faces to make him laugh.

Warmth spread through my chest.

"Man, aren't they adorable? It would almost be enough to make me think about having another one."

"Don't do that."

I got the feeling Owen spoke without thinking.

I caught his eye and raised an eyebrow.

"Clare, I love you, but you were freaking out about the extra work you would have to do when Michael bought a cat. I don't think you would deal well with another child."

I had to give him that one.

"What am I going to do?"

"Talk to your psychologist and get better." Owen said.

"The kids said Owen and Alfie were here this afternoon," Michael said as he lifted the covers and climbed into the bed with me.

He snuggled up to me and I pressed my feet against his shins.

"Holy Crap, your feet are cold!"

He tried to twitch his legs away from me, but I had my feet locked around them. I gave an evil giggle.

Eventually, he extricated his legs and we settled down.

"So," he said, "Owen?"

I had forgotten to answer in the tussle, "Yeah, he came around for a coffee after picking Alfie up this afternoon. You should have seen the kids playing together, it was so cute."

"You seem to be talking to Owen a lot lately."

The comment was meant to sound casual, but I felt an undertone in his voice.

"No more than usual. He's my friend, honey. I talk to him about stuff." I rolled over to face him, "Are you jealous of me talking to another man?"

He wiggled his head, non-committal.

"Oh, baby. There is only room for one main man in my life."

I kissed him and he rolled over, presenting me his back to snuggle into.

"I love you," he said.

"I love you, too."

I plonked a kiss on his back, closed my eyes and waited for sleep.

Chapter Twenty Two

Irony – when thinking about treatment for your anxiety gives you anxiety.

I had been buzzing since lunch time.

My legs bounced wildly and I found my thumbs running over my fingernails when I was sitting idle.

When Doctor Imra had walked into the staff kitchenette I caught her looking at me sideways, like my tension was visible.

I had smiled at her as brightly as I could and rubbed at my sternum when she looked away. The heartburn was back again.

I studied the waiting room of the unfamiliar medical practice. The room was lit with long fluorescent bulbs and was unexpectedly warm despite the lack of windows. Several landscape paintings adorned the walls.

I studied the nearest one.

It was a beach scene, set from the ocean looking back onto the land. A small family roamed along the waterline, the dunes extending in grassy waves behind them.

What is this woman going to think of me? I thought. *Will she think I'm hopeless or useless? Of course she won't. Her job is to see people like you and help them, us, work it out.*

People like me. I sighed. *The crazy people.*

"Clarissa?"

I pulled my unfocussed gaze from the landscape and looked at the woman who had called my name.

Great balls of fire, she looks younger than I am.

I fought to convince myself that her age didn't preclude her qualifications. It was difficult; I swear she could have passed for a sixteen-year-old.

"Call me Clare," I said.

I took her offered handshake and she motioned me into a small room.

"Would you like a cup of tea or cold water?" she asked.

"No thank you, I'm fine."

She invited me to take a seat while she filled her own cup.

I sat down in a chair that was designed to look slick and comfortable, but actually had a back that was way too low and a thin seat cushion.

"Hi Clare," the psychologist (was that right, yeah, the talky one) sat down at the desk, "My name is Rachel, how are you today?"

The woman smiled. Her smile was soft and warm, I wanted to like her.

I decided to be completely honest with her. If I couldn't be honest with my psychologist what hope did I have?

"I'm a little nervous actually. Probably even a little anxious."

Rachel smiled again, "That is a perfectly normal response. I even get a little nervous meeting new clients sometimes.

"Now," she said, putting on a business tone, "Tell me why you think you are here today."

Where do I start? The Big Bang?

I didn't think she'd appreciate my jokes.

"Well, I saw one of the doctors at my work last week because I've been short-tempered and a little off lately. I thought maybe I had low iron, but my iron was normal and Doctor Imra said maybe I had some anxiety."

Rachel nodded, "That does seem to be the case. I've read through the letter from Doctor Imra, she said you have been having some panic attacks and some problems with worrying?"

I nodded.

"Alright," she said, "Usually in the first session I will try to find the cause of some of your worries and if there is time we might be able to go through some strategies as well, okay?"

I nodded. I didn't feel quite up to speaking to her, my nerves were jangling around again. I was half surprised there wasn't an echo of rattling chains through the small room.

"Okay, so, can you think of anything that might be causing you to worry more than usual?"

I frowned and shook my head.

"Alright," Rachel said, "That's fine. I'm going to tell you some things that can often lead to anxiety disorders and I want you to tell me if they might be contributors for you."

"Okay."

"Alright," she said, "We'll start with the easy ones. Have you been sleeping well lately?"

I shook my head.

"Having trouble getting to sleep?"

I nodded.

"Okay," she scrawled on a notepad. "That can be both a cause and a symptom of anxiety problems.

"Have you been feeling particularly stressed? Are you undertaking any new projects, have you had any changes in your life?"

"No, not really. Well, no changes and no more stressed than usual."

Her pen scratched across the paper, "Do you feel under pressure a lot of the time?"

"I'm a working parent. We're like walking pressure cookers."

She laughed gently. "I'm glad to see you have a sense of humour. Have you been having any physical symptoms?"

"I think so." I said, "I've been having headaches and I think I've been getting heartburn."

She nodded, "Okay. Do you have any questions?"

"Why didn't you ask if I'd had any trauma, isn't that usually what causes mental issues?"

"Mental *Health* Issues," Rachel corrected gently. "Not all cases of anxiety are caused by trauma, Clare.

"Your mental health relies on several interlacing factors," she started to draw a little diagram on her notepad, "sleep, hormones, stress, physical activity and your feelings of self-worth all have a role to play in your mood. Positive thinking also has a role, but you can't overcome all of the other factors just by thinking positively."

Huh, that actually all makes sense.

"So, I want to talk you through some things you can do now to help with all of the other factors. First, we'll talk about stress."

I nodded and wondered if I should be taking notes.

"Everyone feels stress, but the way we handle it changes from person to person. Some people are able to go through a stressful situation, handle the burst of adrenaline it gives them and then roll on with their day. Other people take the stress and store it away.

"I'm going to talk you through a little self-awareness activity now, just to help illustrate my point. I'd like you to close your eyes for me."

I followed her instruction.

"Now, we're going to run a self-scan through your body. I'd like you to start with your face; can you feel any tightness in the muscles of your face at all?"

What, how do you feel stuff in your face? I thought harder and realised my forehead was scrunched up, a furrow between my eyes.

I nodded to her and tried to smooth the muscles.

"Good. Now, what about your neck and shoulders?"

My shoulders were hunched up and tight, I drew them away from my ears, stretching out a muscle in my neck as I did so.

"I saw that," I heard a smile in her voice, "Well done. Now your arms?"

My fingers were clenched tightly on the armrests.

Rachel talked me through the rest of my muscle groups and I discovered that my tummy was clenched tight and my thighs were tensed, but at least my toes and ankles were relaxed.

"Alright, so there is something for you to practice," Rachel sent me a sunny smile. "I want you to find some time every day to run through that exercise and practice releasing the tension in those muscles.

"You can also practice some meditation, find somewhere nice and quiet to sit..."

I couldn't stop the snort.

"...I know that might be hard for you with the little ones at home, but you can always practice it with them, they would benefit from some mindfulness activities too.

"Another thing that might help is finding a creative outlet. More research is being done at the moment into the importance of creativity for relieving symptoms of stress and anxiety. Do you have any creative outlets? Drawing, colouring, painting?"

"I crochet?" I posed it as a question as I didn't know whether that counted.

"That sounds promising, what do you crochet?"

I looked at my nails, "I'm crocheting a blanket for someone's baby at the moment, but I don't really like the colours she chose and the pattern is a cow."

Rachel's eyebrows squinched together, "That doesn't sound very rewarding for you. Can you crochet something for yourself, or find something else that feels rewarding when you've finished? Something that feeds your soul."

Something that feeds your soul.

"Do you feel like you get a chance to be yourself?" Rachel asked, "I know that people with young kids often feel like they get lost in all the jobs they have to do. It's important for you to be able to have some time to be *you* for a little while too. Not necessarily every day or even every week, but you need to fill yourself up, too.

"You can't pour from an empty cup."

"So, basically, I need to be selfish once in a while?"

I could work with that.

"It's called *self-care*," Rachel smiled, "But basically, yes."

★　　★　　★

I thought about Rachel's advice as I drove home.

Do something creative.

I did have a favourite creative pastime when I was a teenager, but it wasn't something I had indulged in for many years.

Not since Michael and I had moved in together.

I made a decision and hit the call button on my steering wheel.

"Hello?" The voice came through my car stereo.

"Mum? I want to start practicing again."

Chapter Twenty Three

*Practice makes perfect or so they say, perhaps perfection
will come another day.*

"I'm just ducking to Mum's for a bit. The kids should
be asleep by now."

I gave Michael a kiss and looked at him.

"Mum's?" he asked. "You're going to your Mum's
house?"

"Yeah," I said, "Is that okay?"

I didn't really have the patience to talk it through with
him, or come up with a plausible excuse. I had already
waited over twenty-four hours since making my decision
and any further delays might push me over the edge.

"Sure," he sounded more confused than accepting.

"I'll see you later, don't wait up."

I gave him another peck on the cheek.

Mum only lived a few streets away so I left the car in
the driveway and walked, enjoying the kiss of the cooling
night air on my cheeks. My short hair was fluffed up by the
breeze.

It had taken several weeks, but I had finally gotten
used to the shorter hair style. I had come to like it.

I let myself in to Mum's house without knocking.

"I'm here."

Mum stepped into the corridor and took in my
appearance, "Oh my, did you actually walk? Have I taught
you nothing?"

I frowned at her, "It's a nice night. I had a very
enjoyable time in the fresh air."

She smiled and pressed a kiss to my cheek, "I'm glad."

"Okay, I guess I had better get to work."

"I'm so proud of you." Mum said.

"Calm down. It's not like I'm about to cure world hunger."

"I know, I'm just so glad that you're coming back."

I swear I saw a glint of tears in her eyes.

"Come along, mother dearest, we've got a lot of work to do and I don't think we're going to get it all done tonight."

Mum had kindly agreed to let me use my old bedroom as my work room.

I couldn't freely practice at my own home. Michael would ask too many questions and there would be too great a risk that the kids would stumble upon my materials and who knows what disasters that would lead to.

My room looked much the same as it had when I moved out.

I lived there through my undergraduate degree, so there weren't any embarrassing boy band posters still adorning the walls, but there was an old timetable on the pin board and a cutesy old photo of Michael and me.

I was kissing him on the cheek and someone had taken our photo with a polaroid camera. It might have been Owen.

Dear Owen. He had been messaging me every day to see how I was going. Sending me stupid pictures and memes during the day to make me smile. He was a good friend.

"What's that little smile for?" Mum caught a look at me in the mirror. "Thinking about your husband naked?"

I blushed. "Eww, Mum. It is so wrong of you to talk like that."

"What? I have to live vicariously through someone. It's not like I'm getting any, nor is Nora."

I closed my eyes and suffered a mental sneeze while trying to supress those images.

"I do not need to know anything about your, or Mrs

Corney's, sex life, thank you very much. I feel like I need to bleach my brain."

Note to self: get Mum some Mills and Boon for her birthday. That might save me from another one of those awful conversations.

"I'm disappointed Clare. Sex is a perfectly natural part of adulthood. You really shouldn't feel embarrassed."

"I'm not embarrassed, Mum," I totally was, "I'm just not getting any, okay?"

Mum looked aghast, "What?"

"Look, by the time we've both got all our shit done, there just isn't time. Or our libidos just never quite line up or one of the kids walks in just as things are getting steamy, it just doesn't happen much anymore. Now can we drop the subject and get to work?"

We worked in an awkward silence for a minute. We cleared the surface of the desk and slid it underneath the window where my crystals could charge with the sun or the moon, depending on the elemental. Tonight happened to be a full moon, lucky for me.

"Now then."

I got down on the floor and looked under the bed. My eyes were met with darkness and dust bunnies.

"Hmm."

I fished my phone out of my pocket and turned the flashlight on.

"Jackpot."

An old black briefcase sat in the back corner. I stretched out full length and half shimmied under the queen-sized bed to reach the handle of the case.

I did the worm to get back out, my treasure in hand.

"Alright."

I sat on the edge of the bed and popped the latches. I lifted the lid to find little black velvet bags. Still lined up neatly with a tag on each drawstring.

I felt the stored magic. The call of the crystals energised me.

"Some of them are still charged. After all this time."

"Of course they are." Mum said.

I didn't answer her.

I placed my hands inside the case and scried out the crystals with the most energy.

I pulled out four little bags and tumbled their contents into my hand. Four stones rested on my palm. Red, green, turquoise and black.

They warmed in my hand and fuelled an excitement in me. Unable to hold back any longer, I whispered to the stones.

They began to glow. Four little beacons in the palm of my hand.

I lost myself to myself for a while.

I painted pictures in the air with the light from the crystals. I made multi-coloured fireworks displays. I created the illusion of a garden in the air before us.

Mum watched the display in silence, the light glimmering in her eyes.

The lights began to wane as the crystals were drained of power. First the red light faded, then the turquoise, leaving only dribbles of green and black to weave together.

Only when all the light was out did I take the time to identify the crystals.

Ruby – For action, energy and courage.

Chrysoprase – Personal insight, optimism, acceptance.

Amazonite – Inspiration, expression and balance.

The black was not a crystal at all, but lava stone – for courage and stability.

I laughed lightly and showed the crystals to Mum. "Looks like they knew I would need them."

Mum smiled and squeezed my hand.

We went to work in silence, comfortable silence this time. We set the crystals out in a grid for optimum charging and I followed my intuition for the layout and pattern created.

Seeing the rainbow colours of my crystals set out in state like that brought a lightness to my heart.

My sigh was one of satisfaction when we finished.

"You'll close the curtains for me in the morning?" I

asked.

"Of course," she said.

I plonked another kiss on her cheek, "Thank you, I'll stop by tomorrow to pack them all away."

"You're welcome," she said as she followed me to the door.

"I'm proud of you, Clare." She smiled, this time I was certain there were tears in her eyes, "That light display tonight was beautiful. I wish you could share it with the world."

"Sharing it with you is enough."

We shared a tight hug before I turned to walk home.

"Night, Mum."

The air had cooled considerably and I shivered. I pulled the tails of my draped cardigan up and pulled it tight to my body, tucking my hands into my armpits.

I realised I was hunched and tried to pull my shoulders away from my ears but they migrated back up again in the vain hope that I might be able to keep the bare back of my neck warm.

The loss of feeling in my toes was almost worth it when I turned the corner into my street and was greeted by the full moon rising straight ahead of me.

The great white orb hovered just above the rooftops; the face of craters looked sadly down on me, clear in the cloudless sky.

I forgot what I was doing for a moment and paused to absorb the beauty of the night sky. Shimmering stars, glowing moon and migrating satellites kept me transfixed despite the chill in the air.

A siren sounded behind me, a car alarm going off. The car was too distant for me to see the cause of the screeching, but the alarm jolted me.

I think I'm high on magic.

I shook myself and walked the length of three more houses to reach home.

The front light was on and I studied the front garden critically.

The roses were well past the time they should have

been pruned. The lawn was quite long about the edges, but the pots of petunias alongside the path added some colour and fun to the garden. Mainly from the bright murals Kaylee and Amaya had painted on them.

I looked at my house and I saw hope.

Sure things were a bit crap for me right now, my buds needed pruning and my lawn could do with a trim (double entendre intended), but there was always space for a spot of colour and you could always add a new place for things to grow.

Chapter Twenty Four

What you imagine always ends up being worse than the truth.

"What time did you get home last night?" Michael asked over the rim of his coffee cup.

I carried my toast to the table and sat down.

"Around ten I think."

I crunched into the toast, closing my eyes to enjoy the balance of sweet and savoury given by spreading honey over peanut butter.

"What on earth were you doing with your mother until that late?"

"Just talking. I didn't get there until after eight, it wasn't like I was there half the day."

He grunted and went back to whatever he was reading on his phone.

I started whistling to myself as I opened up my own phone.

"You seem happy this morning," he said.

I studied his comment, turning it over and analysing it in my head.

"I am happy today. What shall we do?"

Unlike when I had used magic a few weeks earlier, where I had drained myself to create the bubble and save the child from injury, using magic stored in the stones energised me.

I felt like I had slept for eleven hours straight, when I had actually just created something beautiful, charged myself under the full moon and slept for eight hours without memorable dreams.

It was lovely.

"I don't know, what do you want to do?"

His voice sounded funny, maybe because the kids had woken up early.

"I can take the kids out for a while and you can have some quiet time if you like."

"Where would you go?"

I took another bite of my toast, "I don't know, they've been wanting to go to the swimming centre for a few weeks, maybe I'll take them there."

He studied my face, "Can you manage them both at the pool on your own?"

"It will be tricky, but I think I'm up to the task."

I had expected he would be pleased to have some time to himself, it doesn't happen very often.

"Fine."

"Michael? Did you want to come swimming with me and the girls?"

"No, it's fine. I'll stay home."

I had misjudged him.

"I'm sorry," I said, "I thought you might like to have some time to yourself. I didn't mean to upset you."

"I'm not upset," he said, leaving the table to put his mug on the sink. "I'll be on the computer, let me know when you go out."

He left me sitting at the table with half a plate of toast and no appetite, wondering what the hell I had done wrong.

★　　★　　★

My mood crunched like a dry egg shell, I hustled the kids to get changed and go swimming.

I sent Owen a quick text.

"Want to come swimming with me and the girls this morning?"

"Sure. Alfie and I would love to join you." his reply came through a few minutes later. "Bea has gone out for coffee with her book club this morning."

"Awesome. We're just getting ready to leave."

147

"Alfie found his bathers as soon as I said 'swim'. We won't be far behind you."

I worried about Michael as I drove to the swimming centre.

Am I shutting him out? I thought I was doing the right thing by not telling him about the anxiety, but maybe I'm being selfish by not sharing my burden.

And then there's the magic. I've kept a part of me separate from him for the whole time we've been together.

Still, it's not that bad, if I told him now it would be like him discovering I was a concert pianist. It isn't like I was a serial killer or anything like that.

I worried at my lip as I drove. I peeled off a piece of dry skin and swore when it tore.

I pulled my lip into my mouth and sucked it.

Man, I actually swore then as well. A real swear word.

Reviewing the last few weeks I realised that my instances of real swear words had actually been growing. *I wonder if that's from my anxiety.*

I pulled in to the car park at the swimming centre to the sounds of a screaming fit from my children.

I turned off the engine and turned on them.

"You two! Cut it out! If you two don't turn start getting along right now we'll go straight home."

Where I will then run away to join the circus and leave you to the tender mercies of your father.

That would make him grumpy.

I started wondering what sort of life I would make for myself if I did run away. Maybe I would live on a beach front and slowly turn into some sort of beach bunyip. I would never wash my hair. It would turn into a dreadlocked, matted mess and I would swim with dolphins and sharks until I became some sort of pseudo-mermaid.

I was pulled from my daydream by Amaya trying her hardest to get run over.

The beep of a car-horn drew me to her plight. She was

standing in the middle of the roadway with a pool noodle around her waist, singing to herself.

"Dude! You're in a carpark, could you pay attention to your surroundings please?"

I could feel my stress levels skyrocketing again. They did my head in.

"Right," I said when I was weighed down with all of my gear, changes of clothes, towels and snacks to stave off the hangries after the swim. "Let's go."

"Mama," Amaya said, "Can you hold my pool noodle."

"Sure, why not." I tucked the piece of tubular foam under my arm.

Somehow I managed to get them to hold my hands as we traversed the car park to the centre.

It was full.

I had once again come during swimming lesson time when three quarters of the pool was sectioned off for classes.

Damn.

"There's nowhere to swim." Kaylee whined.

"There's plenty of room still, let's find somewhere to put our things and then go have our rinse off."

Someone shouted my name from the middle of the pool and I found Owen in the middle, Alfie floating in front of him. He pointed to the side and I spotted Alfie's backpack.

Identifiable as it was one of the personalised ones that you order online. You know, the sort of bag that people who are really organised and plan ahead have.

I tossed our assorted, mismatched bags on the bench.

"Let's go kiddos."

We hustled in to the pool and met Owen in the middle, Alfie swimming neat little laps around him.

Another thing to feel guilty about.

Michael and I had never gotten around to taking our kids for swimming lessons. At least they were starting to learn now. Between the swimming lessons from school and our semi-regular visits to the swimming centre, they were getting there.

"On your own today?" Owen asked.

"Just me and the girls," I said.

He cocked his head questioningly.

"I thought Michael might like to have a morning to himself, but apparently I was wrong."

I thought of the blank look he'd given me when I said we were leaving and a stab of pain pierced my chest.

Apparently, it showed on my face.

"Clare," Owen appealed, "I still think you should tell him."

"I know you do." I didn't want to confess that I had wondered about the wisdom of my decision that morning, too. "I'll ask the psych at my next visit."

Any further attempts at adult conversation were overruled by the raucous activity of our children.

Kaylee and Amaya truly adored Alfie. They turned into little mothers around him. Showing him things and teaching him new words. It was adorable.

Despite that, I still felt an underlying, nagging worry that I had somehow stuffed up with Michael.

Only time would tell.

And time told a rather unpleasant story.

Michael was still in a mood when we got home. I avoided him while I put all of the wet things in the wash, but I did hear the girls babbling to him. Finally, I walked in to the office to ask about his morning.

"Have you eaten?" He asked, before I had a chance to open my mouth.

Given that it was past one and the kids were not screaming messes I thought the answer to that question would have been fairly obvious.

"Yeah, we had chips after swimming. Have you had something to eat?"

"No. I thought you might bring something home for me."

He stomped toward the kitchen without letting me answer.

Great. Happy kids, grumpy husband. I just can't win.

"Would you like me to make you something?" I called out as I followed him.

"No, it's fine. I'll have a pie."

He pulled a pastry from the freezer and stuck it in the microwave. I jumped when he slammed the microwave door closed.

"Okay. Are you alright with the girls for a bit? I need to go to Mum's for a little while."

He grunted.

I took the grunt as a yes. "Okay, I'll see you in a bit then."

I was already in the doorway with my back to him when he spoke again.

"The girls said Owen was at the swimming centre. You seem to spend more time with him than you do with me lately."

I turned to face him slowly. I didn't know what to say.

"Owen is... a good friend. You know that. And the girls love to play with Alfie."

"They also like to play with me."

My stomach tightened.

"I asked if you wanted to come with us."

"After you'd already said you would take them alone. Were you leaving me home so you could spend time with Owen?"

Now I really didn't know what to say. What had gotten in to him? He'd never been jealous, especially not of Owen, who he knew was also married, and completely besotted with Bea.

"You're being ridiculous. I'm going out, I'll see you later."

My stomach roiled as I closed the front door behind me. I didn't slam it, but I wanted to.

How could he be such a prat when I'm going through so much right now. Another little voice chimed in. *Because he doesn't know what you're going through Einstein. Maybe if you told him....*

I'm not telling him.

I'd already had the argument about telling him and I

didn't want to have it again. I was sure I'd had good reason to keep my anxiety to myself.

If only I could stop worrying about his mood for a minute to remember what those reasons were.

Chapter Twenty Five

Going for a walk with children is fifty percent telling them to catch up, fifty percent telling them to slow down and much less relaxing than you thought it would be.

When the sun peeked through the curtains I did what any mature adult would do.

I hid under the covers.

Sleep had been hard to come by again. Michael had firmly given me his back all night and when he rolled over he kept his arms to himself.

No spoon action in our bed last night.

His side of the bed was empty and cold, so he probably hadn't slept well either.

I reached for my phone and pulled it into my private blanket fort.

I had new messages from Owen. A series of memes and a video of baby goats on a trampoline.

He knew I had a soft spot for baby goats.

I tossed the blanket off my head when the air fouled and nearly dropped my phone when I found Michael staring at me.

"Are you having fun in there?"

I wondered how to treat him. *Do I get upset because he was cranky with me all day or do I treat him like I normally do and just pretend it never happened?*

I opted for the latter and showed him the video of the goats.

He cracked a small smile. He tapped the screen and the smile faded.

"From Owen?"

I think I'll have to tread carefully here.

"Yes, he sends me funny videos. As friends do."

Michael sat down on the edge of the bed and leaned over. He placed a hand on either side of my head and studied my face.

"Are we okay?" he asked.

"Yes? Why wouldn't we be?"

"I don't know." He looked sad. "You've just been acting strangely lately and Owen has been around a lot..."

I pulled him down and kissed him. Insecure husband was cute.

"I love *you*. Owen has nothing to do with our relationship."

He smiled softly. "Are you sure?"

"Very."

He leaned forward to kiss me again. The bedroom door thumped open and the children bashed into our bedroom and jumped on the bed.

"Mummy, I'm hungry." Amaya said.

"Daddy, can I have a chocolate?" asked Kaylee.

Michael looked at me and shook his head. "We're raising heathens. Right you two, off to the kitchen. I'll make you toast and then I'll think about chocolate."

"Noooo." I cried, "No chocolate after breakfast!"

"Just today, it's Sunday," Michael's receding voice said. "The rules don't apply on Sunday."

"What's chocolate?" the little voice came from near my feet.

"People food," I told the kitten. "Bad for cats."

The kitten walked up and rubbed its head against my outstretched hand.

"How long were you sleeping down there, little one?"

The kitten started to purr, "Some time after you went to bed, some time before you woke up."

Very specific. Thank goodness cats never had to be relied upon to provide alibis, they were terrible with time.

"We need to find a name for you don't we? I can't keep calling you 'kitten'."

The little creature rolled and presented me his tummy to scratch. Predictably, I only rubbed a few times before he started attacking my hand.

"Ow," I said.

He started licking my hand in apology.

"A name, little one. Do you have one?" I asked.

"Littlest," he said promptly.

He clearly had a very imaginative mother.

The girls had been tossing up names for him all week but nothing had stuck. Somehow, their suggestions of Sparkles, Mr Glitter, Shimmer and Sandra just didn't quite fit.

"What about Glitz then? No, you make me think of Broadway. I'm going to call you Razzle, like 'Give 'em the old Razzle Dazzle'. How does that sound?"

He purred.

There was one thing in my life sorted out and I hadn't even gotten out of bed yet.

Winning!

"Mama?" Amaya's voice broke into my musing.

"Yeah, baby?"

"Can we go for a walk to the playground?"

I checked my watch. 2:30PM. There was still plenty of time to go out before dinner.

"Sure. Does Kaylee want to come too?"

"Yep."

"Okay, can you go find Daddy and see if he wants to join us?"

"Yep."

She skipped from the deck to go and find Michael, singing as she went.

She was singing 'Bang, Bang' by Nikki Minaj. Totally appropriate for a five year old. Not.

I drank the last dregs of my tea and braced myself for the walk.

The park was about 400m from home, but could take fifteen minutes on a bad day. I prayed today would not be a bad day.

"Kaylee!"

I checked every room of the house before I found her in her bedroom, lying face down on her bed.

"Kaylee? Honey? What's wrong?" I knelt down so my face was at her level.

"Mmmf, mmf, mmf mmf!"

Amazing!

"I can't hear you sweetheart, you need to pull your face away from the pillow."

"I wanted to ask you if we could go to the park, but we played rock, paper, scissors and Amaya won, so she got to ask!"

Kaylee burst into tears.

Honestly. What the hell could I do to make that situation better?

"Oh dear. I can see why you are upset." *Because you didn't get things your way,* "but, the good thing is, Amaya asked and I said yes. So we can go as soon as you and your sister are ready.

"Could you choose some shoes please and get ready to go?"

"No!"

I took a deep breath to stop myself from breathing fire at my daughter. Literally.

"Okay then, if you don't want to get ready, you can stay home with Daddy."

Michael poked his head around the doorway, "I'm not staying home. I want to go to the playground. You'll be staying home to look after Razzle."

I rubbed my hand up over my face. I felt the buzzing magic from my hand discharge and send the hair on that side of my head into a frizz.

At least I could use magic without suffering debilitating magical whiplash thanks to my cleansed and charged crystals. I left Michael to negotiate with Kaylee and swiped the opposite hand through my hair, collecting the static energy and storing it in a crystal on a chain around my neck.

I had specifically chosen a stone capable of storing my

run away magic. I hadn't had to take action like that since I was a hormone-crazed teenager.

What's old is new again.

Amaya was sitting by the front door. She was wearing shoes, matching socks and a hat and was putting on sunscreen.

"Good job, Amaya. Very sun smart."

I filled a bag with snacks and drinks and we waited for Michael and Kaylee.

"Just head off without us," Michael called when there was a lull in the screaming.

I didn't wait to be told twice.

"Let's go, Kiddo!"

"Let's go, Mummo!"

I smiled and we started walking.

The park could be reached by turning left or right at the end of our driveway. The path to the left was slightly longer. I let Amaya choose which way to go. She chose the right-hand path.

We stopped at least every ten metres.

Amaya found a butterfly, an interesting flower, had a rock stuck in her shoe. There were so many stops along the way that Michael and Kaylee, who left after us and took the longer route, were at the playground well before we were.

"We beat you," Kaylee said, full of smiles now she had something to gloat about.

I smiled wanly.

The walk had taken its toll. Instead of being a relaxing walk, I had grown impatient with Amaya as the walk went on.

I had stuff to do, washing to fold, floors to mop, I didn't need to spend half of my afternoon walking less than half a kilometre to a playground.

The child was hopeless. Completely without hope.

I sat on a swing and picked up a gentle rhythm. I checked my body and realised my shoulders were tight. I rolled them a few times to release some tightness in the muscle.

Why am I so wired? That 9v battery was back, the low charge coursing through my system and putting me on edge.

With a start, I realised it was the anxiety. *Was that what Rachel and Doctor Imra were trying to tell me? Anxiety keeps me on edge?*

I watched a pigeon cross the park, Amaya ran over to it. The pigeon pooped and flew away.

It brought to mind the fight or flight response. If the pigeon was bigger and Amaya was smaller, maybe the pigeon would have fought instead of flown.

A momentary image of Amaya being chased through the playground by a pigeon as tall as the swing set flitted through my mind.

Jokes aside, I turned the fight or flight concept over in my mind.

Adrenaline is released when you need to run away from something. It gives you a burst of energy to get away and in the case of pigeons it also makes you poop, because it's wise to lighten the load before taking off.

Was there too much adrenaline in my system? Was that the chemical imbalance Rachel had been talking about?

I pulled out my phone and consulted Doctor Google.

I skimmed over the first article that popped up. Terms that popped out included that you breathe faster, your heart beats rapidly and you tend to sweat under the influence of adrenaline.

Well that makes sense.

The article also mentioned that you can have an adrenaline rush at night when you think about stresses from the day, which means you're all hyped up and can't sleep.

The section on controlling adrenaline mentioned meditation, deep breathing and yoga. Which, now I thought about it, were all things Rachel had suggested. Fancy that.

Another thing that drew flags in the article was mention of the 'stress hormone' cortisol.

I read that cortisol is important in general as it gives you energy to face challenges, but too much causes anxiety. Reducing cortisol levels was generally the same as reducing adrenaline levels, plus a little exercise and social connections. That was handy; at least I only had to remember one treatment plan.

So I needed to find time to meditate, exercise and socialise.

Easy? Not so much.

My level of stressors had skyrocketed by the afternoon.

Fights between the kids, Michael still not quite talking to me, all the craft supplies spread out in the lounge room less than fifteen minutes after I had vacuumed the floor in there.

The 9v battery felt like it grown big enough to start a car instead of just powering the smoke detector.

I decided to try one of the stress reducing techniques and meditate.

"What are you doing, Mama?" Amaya asked.

I could feel them both looking at me as I sat on the lounge with my eyes shut.

"I'm trying to meditate, baby." I tried to dampen my snappy reaction and kept my tone even.

"What's meditate?" Kaylee asked.

"It's where you sit quietly and try to relax."

"What's relaxing?" Amaya asked.

"The opposite of this," I grumbled.

I stopped trying.

"Why don't you go jump on the trampoline?" I suggested.

The girls ran outside with a chorus of hoots and hollers.

Footsteps came thumping down the hall just as I managed to clear my mind again.

"Mama?" Amaya asked, "Will you come out and watch us?"

I sighed. "Where's Daddy, will he watch you?"

"I can't find him. I think he's pooping."

"Of course he is."

I would not be held responsible for my actions if he found my chocolate stash.

Or his actions if he found my spell book.

I say 'spell book' but it's more of a magical journal. A log of spells performed rather than spells learned.

Manipulating magic should be instinctual, not learned. If you tried to learn it all from a book, success wouldn't be impossible, but it would be hard to come by. It's much better to read situations and manage them than to plough through like a sledgehammer in half-set cement.

I grabbed a cushion from the outdoor sofa and settled myself on the lawn in a tailor's seat. I was close enough to the trampoline to see the girls but far enough away to get some peace.

I closed my eyes and started the meditation attempts afresh.

I listened to the sounds of the birds, the rustling leaves, the laughs of the children, the tread of heavy feet on the deck.

I sighed again.

"What you doing?" Michael's voice interrupted my peace.

"I'm *trying* to medicate, ugh *meditate,* but it seems everyone in this house is conspiring against me!'

"Why?"

I splayed my fingers and rubbed my forehead. I counted to three.

"Because I heard that it can reduce stress."

"What are you stressed about?"

All the stupid questions you keep asking me!

I tried to keep a lid on my temper, it wasn't *entirely* his fault.

"I don't know! Everything! All the stuff I have to do in daily life. Everything I do at work and then all the things I have to do at home. The children ignoring what I ask them to do at least eighty per cent of the time."

"Huh. So how will meditating help? Wouldn't it be

better to just do the work?"

I don't think the heat would have travelled through my body faster if I'd sat on a fire ant nest.

"Let's see, maybe because there aren't actually enough hours in the day to do all the damn jobs I have to do. Also, I'd like to try and stay semi-sane, so I'm not shouting at the kids all the time!"

Yep, I was shouting at him instead.

He held his hands up, palm toward me and took a step back.

"I'll take the kids inside then so you can have your peace."

He called the girls without any further conversation. He told them Mummy needed some time to calm down. The burning in my chest fizzled up at his words.

I sighed. I wanted to be left alone, but I didn't want to *be* alone.

Stupid, contrary emotions.

I closed my eyes and hoped for third time lucky on my meditation attempts.

I listened to the leaves in the trees. Their soft susurrus made me think of Kaylee and Amaya telling secrets to each other.

I smiled as I thought of them. I wondered what they were doing. The house was quiet, maybe they had gone out. I thought of all the horrible things that could happen. A car accident. A kidnapping. A broken leg from falling off a swing.

Beads of sweat formed on the back of my neck and I realised that my breathing had quickened.

I focussed on breathing steadily again and stamped on the anxious thoughts.

I felt a light breath of wind fluffing my hair. Rainbow lorikeets flew overhead, chattering away.

Their screeches sounded like the cries of children. I thought of all the children stuck in war torn countries. Syria and Palestine. My stomach clenched as I thought about just how damn lucky I was to have been born in the country I lived in now. I thought of the children in detention at the behest of my government and bile rose in my throat.

How could they be so cruel?

I jolted when a weight landed on my shoulder.

A small cheech announced that Dash was my new companion.

I slowed my breathing again.

Man, I never thought this would be so hard.

Dash grabbed a lock of my hair and twiddled it in his beak.

The soft pull and fall of pieces of my hair distracted me.

"Dash!"

"Clare, what do you do?"

"I'm trying to relax!"

"What is?"

I closed my eyes and took a deep breath as I worked out how to frame an explanation in a manner the bird would understand.

"Like at the end of the day, before you settle to sleep, you sit with Eneya and groom each other. You enjoy each other's company."

I felt the weight on my shoulder shift. "Where is company?"

"Humans do it differently."

I wondered if it would be better to meditate with someone else. Maybe even with Michael, resting on the couch and playing with his hair.

Except I didn't know if we were talking.

"I will be your company," the little bird said.

I smiled one of my first real smiles for the day, "Thank you, Dash."

"But go there. Lean on the not-tree, you look twisted."

He was right, my back was getting sore, I wasn't strong enough to sit straight for a long period of time. I moved to lean my back against the verandah post.

Dash wobbled on my shoulder a little as I moved, but kept his perch.

I sat and he began grooming my hair.

I focussed on the weight of him on my shoulder. The movement of my hair. The little crunching sounds his beak made. Every now and then a little puff of his breath would hit my neck, or his feathered face would brush my ear.

My breathing stayed steady and even. My heart slowed and I stopped noticing its thundering. I held the troubling thoughts at bay.

I opened my eyes when the galah nibbled gently on my earlobe.

The sky was darkening and the evening chill had begun.

"What is it?" I asked.

"Your family. They ready meal."

I caught a waft of a tomato sauce and guessed that Michael had made bolognaise.

"Thanks Dash." I pressed a kiss to his head.

He nuzzled my chin, then flew away.

I watched him fly, up into the sky and around the gum trees.

I had a sudden yearning to lift myself up and ride the wind with him.

It was intensified by the sounds of shouting inside the house.

I lifted my weary bones from the ground. My bum was numb again, but at least I wasn't emotionally wrung out. I felt slightly lighter than I had before my meditation session, the background buzz in my muscles felt like the battery was nearly flat.

I stepped into the kitchen to the sight of the children sitting quietly at the table. Spaghetti sauce was smeared across their faces – Amaya had some on the top of her ear – but they were eating.

Warmth – not the heartburn kind – spread through my chest and my shoulders released tension I didn't realise had sprung up.

Michael looked up when he heard the door and smiled at me.

"Dinner, my love?" he gestured toward the bowl of

pasta and glass of wine set at my place at the table.

I crossed the room and kissed him.

"Thank you. Let me just grab my phone and I'll join you."

I had left my digital tether in the lounge room.

My serenity was shattered when I entered the room.

Apparently, my half hour of solitude came at a high price – the lounge room was an absolute tip.

Chapter Twenty Six

Just because you can, doesn't mean you should.

I woke to a kitten in the face again.

"Food, Mama?" He purred.

"For me or you? Have I taught you how to turn on the coffee machine yet?"

"Coffee?"

I pulled his lanky body to my chest and scratched his tummy.

He purred.

"I'll show you the coffee machine. Come on."

Michael snored on behind me.

I ignored him.

I carried the kitten as I padded to the kitchen. I showed him the coffee machine.

"This one here, do you want to try?"

I put Razzle on the bench and pointed to the button. He cowered back, uncertainty in his aura.

"What is it?" I asked.

"Purr Mama said, don't touch the human things."

I smiled and rubbed his head. "Good boy. Some human things can be dangerous for cats. You're right; I shouldn't make you do it."

I turned the coffee machine on myself and picked Razzle up. I stopped for the tin of cat food, then carried him into the laundry to give him his breakfast.

I put him down and watched him eat. His shoulder blades poked up from behind his head, sharp and pronounced.

He was still a baby, it wasn't fair for me to get him doing household chores. Not particularly wise either. Who knew what Michael would think if he found the cat making my coffee one morning.

The lack of opposable thumbs would make it a little tricky for him too.

I went back to bed, it was only 5:30AM – Razzle had woken me marginally later than had become usual.

I snuggled into Michael's back and grabbed my phone.

There was a message from Owen already.

"FFS, this child!"

It was timestamped at 5:20.

"Alfie still rising with the sun?"

"The sun?! The sun?! I just looked out the window and I did not see the sun."

I snort laughed. Owen before caffeine had a black sense of humour.

"According to my Google search, the sun will be up at 5:51, it's not all that far away."

"My child may not live to see it." Owen typed.

"Owen, go make yourself a coffee. You get a little 'Lord of Hell' before caffeine."

My phone went silent and I imagined that Owen was pottering around his kitchen. He would turn on the coffee machine, but see to Alfie's breakfast before brewing.

I switched to my regular morning phone routine; email, Facebook, puzzles. On paydays I also checked the bank accounts and moved all the money about.

I sighed and snuggled in to Michael's back. I missed our easy banter.

It was hard to tell exactly when our relationship had changed, but it was probably sometime after Amaya was born. Somewhere in there, we lost ourselves in the hustle of parenting.

So much time was now spent on the kids or the house that we didn't have much time for each other. I felt an ache in my chest that wasn't heartburn or happiness.

I was sad.

Sad for what we had become when we had been so much more.

My phone dinged and drew me out of my morose musings.

I rolled over and Michael woke enough to roll with me. He threw his arm over my body and pulled me in close. My body hummed where our naked skin touched.

He gave me comfort.

I pulled up my phone.

"5:49. Still no sign of the sun, but the son is too bright."

He had attached a picture of Alfie, beaming over his bowl of Weet Bix.

I chuckled.

"What's that?" Michael's voice was muffled by the pillow and sleep.

"Nothing," I said, "Just Owen."

"What time izzit?"

"Ten to six. I'll go have my shower. Will you come in when your alarm goes off?"

He grunted.

Michael was quiet over breakfast.

This wasn't particularly unusual for a Monday morning. We both spent our breakfast time on Monday planning our week. I generally triaged all the tasks on the Mother Load and Michael would plan the accounts he needed to review.

There was a time when I would have discussed that with him, but that was back in the day when we worked for the same accounting firm. Now we had to more strictly abide by the terms of client privacy and he couldn't tell me about his accounts.

He read the news after finishing breakfast and drank his coffee in further silence.

"Michael?" I hesitated as I waited for him to look up from his tablet.

He didn't speak, just pierced me with his gaze.

"Are you okay?"

"I'm fine," he said.

His tone didn't offer an opening for further conversation.

"Okay."

I thought about his weird behaviour while I made lunch for everyone.

Even though we didn't necessarily have time to spend with one another, we always offered affection when the opportunity arose. A casual smack on the bottom, or a kiss in passing were common in our house.

We may not be able to have a conversation about anything other than the bowel habits of our children, but we always had time to show we cared about each other.

I chewed the inside of my lip as I worried. I wondered when the change had happened. I had been so drawn in on myself lately that I couldn't remember the last time I had initiated contact with him.

What if this stupid anxiety thing has broken my marriage?

The string of thoughts that followed was pretty predictable. If we broke up, who would have the kids? Where would we live? He could stay here with the kids and I could live at Mum's. I could be up and around every morning before they woke up. Maybe they wouldn't even need to know we'd split until way down the line.

My mind ran off with the scenario. My stomach clenched and my neck felt clammy. Sweat soaked into my shirt.

"Are they done?" Michael pointed to Kaylee and Amaya's lunchboxes.

"Huh?" I didn't process the words immediately. "Yeah, they're ready."

I looked at him with the notion that we had already separated in my mind and I was surprised to find him talking to me.

"Are you okay, Clare?" his gaze flicked across my face.

"Yeah," I said weakly.

"You barely touched your breakfast."

I looked at the table to see one and a half slices of

toast left on my plate. "I forgot about it."

His brow furrowed. "You what? Clare, it's not like you to skip a meal. I'm pretty sure Amaya got her hangry genes from you."

"I'm fine," I said again, mentally searching for my lost appetite, again.

"If you say so. But if I see you skipping meals again, I'm going to book you an appointment to see one of your GPs."

I kissed him on the lips. He looked surprised. And he tasted like peanut butter.

"Thank you." I said.

"What for?"

"For caring, even when you're grumpy with me."

There was an email from Doctor Imra waiting for me when I got into the office. She asked me to see her when I had a moment.

As it happened, her door was open when I walked past to make my coffee.

"Would you like a cuppa?" I asked from her doorway.

"Yes," Her voice was deep with yearning.

I made coffee for both of us and returned to her office.

I closed the door with my foot and passed the good doctor her coffee.

"So," she said, "You had the appointment with Rachel last week?"

I nodded. I took a sip of my coffee and burned my tongue.

"How do you think that went?"

My stomach roiled as I wondered what I was meant to say.

Do I say it went well? I think it went well. We talked a bit, she gave me some ideas, I left. That's good, isn't it?

"Good?"

Doctor Imra smiled. "It sounded like you were asking me then. Are you sure it was good?"

I shielded myself with my coffee cup. "I think so?"

She raised one of the perfect arches above her eye and

I let my shoulders drop.

"I don't know, it was weird." I said, "I've never seen a psychologist before. We talked about my symptoms. She told me that not one thing leads to anxiety, it's a lot of things rolled up in one. She gave me some ideas on how to handle it."

Doctor Imra nodded and blew on her coffee to cool it before taking a tentative sip. My scalded tongue screeched at me. *Look, that's how you're meant to do it, blow on it first you foolish woman!*

"Have you been able to use any of the techniques?"

"I meditated yesterday and I tried some creative stuff on Friday. The creative side really helped, the effects of the meditation lasted until I went inside."

Doctor Imra smiled, "I know what you mean there. What do you do that's creative?"

Shopkins, I walked right into that one.

"I paint." In a manner of speaking.

There was a point. I wondered if I could turn my light shows into pictures. People would probably pay squillions, especially if they knew the way they were really created.

Best not let that thought run away with you.

"Oh, that's so good, I'd love to see some of your work sometime. I can't paint peanuts."

Yeah, that's never going to happen.

I smiled at her muddled metaphor, then wondered on the source of the correct one. Sayings are weird.

"Oh, really, I can't paint either. Truthfully, Kaylee does a better job than me, I really just make blobs on the page, but I do find it relaxing."

"Good for you."

It was starting to feel like another psychology session.

"Thanks for the chat." I stood and moved to the door.

"Anytime," she said, "Take care, Clare."

"Thanks, Doctor Imra. I'll try."

"Mama, are you meditating again?"

"I'm trying to," I ground out.

Amaya had managed to get right up in my face before

asking.

The sun brought late afternoon warmth into the backyard and the children were meant to be playing on their trampoline. Or in their cubby. Or basically anywhere that didn't involve bothering me.

I had bribed them with ice blocks to leave me alone.

Somewhere, very deep down, I was sure there was a pang of guilt that I should be paying attention to, but I didn't.

Kaylee joined us.

"Can we try too?" She asked.

I wanted to tell them to go away and leave me alone. This was my time and I needed it, but I couldn't bring myself to be quite so cold.

"Sure, why not."

"When we have quiet time at school, we listen to music," Amaya said.

"Really? That sounds like fun."

I closed my eyes and tried to block them out.

"Yeah," added Kaylee, "Can we listen to some music on your phone?"

I sighed heavily, "Sure, why not. What sort of music would you like to listen to?"

"When we're at school, Miss Tylee plays music with no words." Amaya informed me.

"That narrows it down."

My children were definitely not up to interpreting my verbal irony.

"Yeah, that's really pretty." Kaylee added.

I found a meditation soundtrack and turned the volume up on my phone.

Maybe if it's loud enough, it will drown out any noise the kids make.

"Okay, so you need to sit or lay down somewhere, and you need to be comfortable, because you'll need to stay still for a little while."

The children accepted the instruction. Amaya leaned on the other balcony rail and Kaylee lay down on the grass.

After fifteen minutes, three position changes, one tussle for space and two trips to the toilet (both Amaya), the children were finally able to sit still.

By the end of it, I think the five minutes of actual meditation time may have negated the fifteen minutes of stress leading up to it.

Well, there was twenty minutes well wasted. I would have been better off with my Sudoku.

Michael was in the kitchen when I hauled my numb bum off the ground – you'd think that with so much padding it wouldn't be numb half so often.

He turned from the fridge when the door banged behind me.

"It looked like you three were having fun out there."

I closed my eyes, "'Fun' is not the word I would use."

"Nice and relaxing?" His eyes crinkled.

"Did you see the whole session or just the last twenty seconds?"

"I saw the bit where Amaya was picking her nose while you and Kaylee had your eyes shut."

"Eeewww," I tossed an oven mitt at his head.

He tossed it back at me, then followed the action up by pacing across the kitchen to hem me in against the bench.

He growled at me, then kissed me.

I laughed and tried to escape the pen of his arms.

"Let me go, let me go!" I giggled.

"Never!" he said.

He moved his hands from the bench to tickle my sides. I shrieked and squirmed. I whacked unseeing at his arms and slapped his chest.

We were both laughing by the time the kids came in to see what was happening.

We both looked up to see the kids in the door, expressions of worry and confusion on their little faces.

Michael and I turned mock dead pan faces to the children. We looked back at each other.

"You know what this means," he said.

I nodded sombrely, "New targets."

"I'll take the big one, you take the little one."

With that we were off, shouting and thumping our way through the house. Chasing the children as they led us a merry chase and then tickling them until they had the hiccups.

I was panting by the time we finished and my grin was so broad it hurt my face.

I heard a little mewling whimper from the corner of the lounge room and realised that we had frightened the life out of Razzle.

"Oh, Razzle," I said, "I'm sorry! We didn't mean to scare you. We just play noisy games sometimes."

The children immediately calmed down, the occasional hiccup the only thing to break the silence as we tried to coax the kitten out again.

Michael offered to cook the dinner while we talked the cat out of his corner.

I asked the cat to stay shy a little while longer. Any excuse to get out of domestic chores works for me.

★　　★　　★

I giggled.

"What?" Michael looked up.

I was stretched out on the couch with my feet in his lap, stealing his body warmth.

I showed him the video. It was a dog in a tutu. He didn't laugh.

What sort of monster have I married that doesn't laugh at a dog in a tutu?

The video finished and my phone popped back to the messenger screen.

"Owen sent that to you?"

It sounded like an accusation.

"Yeah?" I wasn't sure what my answer should be.

He went silent and sullen. And stopped rubbing my feet.

"What's wrong with that?" I asked.

"Nothing. Nothing," he said.

He moved my feet to the couch and stood up.

Apparently, it was his turn to leave the room in a huff.

"I'm going to bed. Good night."

He didn't even go to the effort of kissing me before he left the room.

Tears pricked my eyes. *What the heck is up with him?*

My phone dinged and I ignored it. I stared at the end of the couch and ran over our exchanges since he'd gotten home from work.

We'd had fun, he'd cooked dinner, the kids had a bath, they went to bed.

There hadn't been any shouting, we hadn't disagreed.

We'd been sitting comfortably until I showed him the video.

Then he saw the video had come from Owen.

He doesn't have a thing about me talking to Owen does he?

Surely he wouldn't. He couldn't.

We'd both known Owen forever.

It must have been something he'd seen on his phone just before. I mean, he hadn't even laughed at that dog in the tutu.

I began to worry.

I played with my fingernails. My mind flicked to the same story it had played the other night. Michael and I separated. The children becoming emotional wrecks. Me having a complete, proper, nervous breakdown.

I was breathing heavily. My chest hurt. My fingers tingled.

I needed... I needed to talk to someone.

Who?

Not Owen. I had relied on him too much lately, and that is what had gotten me into this particular mess.

Trin? No, she had her own stuff to deal with.

Mum? Yeah, Mum might be able to help.

My fingers tingles were getting stronger. A fizz of magic surged up with every beat of my heart.

I had to get through to her quickly.

I didn't want to get off the couch to walk over. I couldn't summon the energy to transport my body. I stole a leaf out of Mum's book.

I closed my eyes and tried to focus on Mum's house in my mind.

I was headed for an out-of-body experience, similar to the trick I'd played with Dash a few days earlier. However, where I had been able to focus on Dash and transfer my consciousness straight into his body, this time I had to work a little harder.

In my mind, I saw Mum's house in real time. The image was fainter and blurrier than in real life, an auric shadow.

I flexed my fingers, but the house grew fuzzier.

I focussed harder, but the picture completely dissolved.

I opened my eyes.

That's never happened before.

My heart was still racing. My chest was burning, the familiar sick taste in my mouth.

My body was tense. *Maybe that's the problem.*

I closed my eyes and took some meditative breaths before trying again.

The picture of Mum's house reappeared.

This time when I focussed, the walls formed dull black lines with faint imprints of warmth and colour. Slim threads of colour ran through house; the memories of humans, hung like a hint of perfume in the air.

I breathed out in relief.

Two sections glowed brilliantly white; the places where my mother and I stored our crystals.

Finally, I found what I was looking for, the bright glow of my mother's aura. She was sitting at her kitchen table.

I memory mapped the room to find what I needed.

Mum had a picture of me in every room of the house, for just this purpose.

Magically abled beings can transfer their consciousness into another living creature. For most of the more intelligent species, this can only be done with their permission.

Granny Weatherwax was right when she said bees

were the hardest to occupy.

In addition to that, we can also slip our minds inside a picture of ourselves.

This skill isn't quite as necessary in the age of mobile phones as it was centuries ago, but it is still a nicer, more personal way to communicate.

"Hello, Clare."

Mother didn't even look up from her tea leaves.

"Hi Mum."

I knew her better than to be surprised.

"You took your time," she said, "I felt the ripples of your magic several minutes ago."

That my portrait had been moved to the dining table directly in front of her gave the truth to her statement. She loved me, but not enough to leave a picture of me in the middle of her dining table.

"I had a little trouble." I confessed.

"Yes, I felt that too. What's up?"

I sighed, "Michael isn't talking to me."

Mum looked up and locked eyes with my chemically formed likeness.

"Why not?"

"I don't know," I let my misery infuse my voice. "If I did know I would fix it."

"Have you told him about your anxiety yet?"

"No," my tone would have made a sullen teenager proud.

Mum sighed, "Maybe you should.

"Even non-magical people can sense changes in your aura, you know that. Michael has probably noticed the shift in you subconsciously. He may have even noticed some of your anxiety. Remember the other week when I said your aura was a mess?"

I nodded.

"Well, it's even worse now. It always does that when you are working on something emotionally. Your mental injury may fester away without spreading when it is left alone, but when you try to fix it... It's like you've spread the damage, the infection, out to every part of you.

"It's like the chicken pox virus. It hides away in your nerves for years before it can reactivate and infects your entire system. Once it's active, your body can fight it again."

"Chicken pox comes back as shingles, Mum. I've seen people come in to work with shingles. It's a horrific condition and there's no cure. People just have to live through the blisters and hope they don't get neuralgia."

"Exactly!" Mum said. "You have to make it a bigger problem in order to get over it."

"I'm not sure that's sound psychological advice."

"I graduated from the school of life."

"Wouldn't you only graduate from the school of life when you die?"

Did I put the idea of Mum dying out into the Universe?

A felt a jolt in my physical body like a bucket of ice water had been tipped on it. A cold hand gripped my neck, although there was no-one there. My stomach clenched. My hold on the picture wobbled as my body called for my spirit to return.

"Clare!" Mum said, "Calm down! What was that all about?"

I didn't speak for a few minutes, trying to soothe my spirit and body to hold the connection.

"I'm okay."

"Clare, your anxiety must be on a hair trigger. You're primed and ready for meltdown at the smallest thing. You need help."

"I know I need help!" I snapped. "I'm getting help. I'm trying to improve myself."

"Clare," Mum's voice gentled. "You don't need to *improve* yourself, you need to *heal* yourself. It isn't as easy as it sounds. You need to be gentle on yourself. And you should tell Michael. Within the next three days. Or I might just tell him myself."

"Tell Michael what though? Looking after you and our children have turned me into an anxious wreck?" I gave a snort of laughter.

"That might work. Or you could say that you've been holding yourself together so fiercely that your grip is starting to slide and you need to slacken it off a bit. That might mean that you become like a half set jelly for a while, but you'll come good again."

"I'd prefer not to compare myself to jelly to my husband if it's all the same to you. There are certain parts of my anatomy that already resemble that remark much too closely for my comfort."

Mum smiled, "I'm glad you still have your sense of humour."

At least Mum got me.

Chapter Twenty Seven

Just as you think it's starting to settle, the hippo spins his tail and the s&t is well and truly stirred.*

"Kaylee, will you please just eat your toast?" I was not caffeinated enough to argue.

"But it's too crunchy," she whined.

I growled, "It's cooked exactly the same way as I do it every day, just eat it!"

I felt a stab of guilt at raising my voice at her, but really, how much could I be reasonably expected to face before 7AM?

She was saved from further ire by Amaya's waking siren call.

My coffee mug was halfway to my mouth. I put it down without taking a sip.

Razzle chased me down the corridor, running between my feet and trying to trip me.

"Argh, Razzle!"

The kitten skittered away.

I thunked the door to the girl's room open and came close to toppling again as my foot caught in a toy car. I moved to lean on the wardrobe so I could shake the car off.

My hand missed the wardrobe and I fell for real. Amaya's shrieking was still ringing in my ears as I went down.

Luckily, Kaylee had tossed her blanket onto the floor when she got up (something I usually berate her for) and it absorbed most of the impact. I narrowly missed whacking my head on the bedside table.

I let out a real swear.

Amaya stopped shrieking and asked, "Are you okay, Mama?"

I didn't answer as I surveyed my body.

A sharp pain in my hip was a doll. My knee was cushioned by a stuffed toy. Munk Munk was staring into my face from a supine position similar to mine.

"Mama?" Amaya asked.

"Yeah, baby. I'm okay."

Weary, but okay.

The only real injury I sustained seemed to be a pulled muscle on the underside of my arm.

Lucky.

My fingers tingled.

Where were you when I was falling?

What happened to instinctual magic saving you when you needed it?

I gave in to the tingling and let the magic run to my injuries and relieve the ache.

Paracetamol had nothing on magic for pain relief. Magic was much more addictive though.

"Well, that's a wild start to the day."

I rolled onto my knees and made Amaya shuffle back in her bed.

"Let me in."

I climbed up and snuggled under the blanket with her.

It was warm and toasty. Her squishy little face was close to mine. Her breath puffed on my face.

"Time to get up, little one."

"Nooo." Her voice was low.

"I know, I know. I didn't want to get out of bed either," I rubbed her cheek, "Sadly, though, I need to get ready for work."

"No, Mama. I want you to stay here with me."

Her little arms snaked out around the back of my neck and she clasped her hands over her wrists.

"I know, baby." A sudden warmth spread through my chest. A puddle of melting chocolate, full of warmth and endorphins. "Me too."

Surprisingly, I meant it.

Staying in bed with my kids all day would be great. As long as they didn't get bored or scratch me with their talons, I mean, toenails.

Still, Kaylee had woken up early and was ready for school – whenever she finally finished her toast – so I had a little time to snuggle with Amaya.

I subsided and snuggled up to her again. I brushed my nose on hers, kissed her little sniffer, rubbed out foreheads.

She was exceptionally sweet early in the morning.

Naturally, after the cuddle time, I was horrifically delayed.

I spent way too long in bed with Amaya. Kaylee still hadn't eaten her toast when we left an hour later and was in a grump because I wouldn't make her a new batch that was less 'toasty'.

Amaya flat out refused to eat.

And Michael had left before I'd climbed out of bed.

Without giving me a kiss.

One day of silent treatment after Monday's video debacle was rough. The second day had been demoralising, and it looked like we were merrily rolling into day three.

Worse, I remembered Mum's threat to tell him about my anxiety if I hadn't told him within three days of our late night, magically-assisted, chat.

If she was precise, which she usually was, I had a little over twelve hours to tell him about my anxiety and possibly about my magic.

A particularly hard task when he wasn't talking to me.

I sighed.

"What's up?" Amy was in the doorway to my broom closet of an office.

"Nothing," I said, then, wanting to be honest, "Well, lots of things, but it would take too long to explain."

I caught her shrug when I turned around.

181

"I know that feeling," she said.

"Adulting sucks sometimes."

She offered me a fist bump, "Ain't it the truth, at least we can drink though."

I smiled, "There is that."

"Coffee?"

"No, I'm good. Thanks."

I wanted to sigh again, but I decided to keep it in this time.

I sent a text message to Michael, "How's your day going?"

It took him half an hour to reply.

Half an hour where my stomach tightened by degrees, the sweat patches on my shirt grew and my heartburn increased.

"Fine."

That did nothing to lower my stress levels.

I messaged Owen instead.

"He's still not talking to me."

"What? Who?" Owen's reply came through while I was on the phone.

I was foolish enough to try and type and talk at the same time. I didn't end up doing either very well.

"Michael. He's not been talking about appointment bookings."

"What?"

I read my previous message, dammit.

"Whoops. Michael hasn't spoken to me since Monday night. I thought I told you."

I tried to get some work done instead of focussing on the little blue dots.

"No, you did not. You just went silent on me and have barely said anything since then. If you didn't start talking today I was going to come and hunt you down after school tonight."

"That would not have helped."

"Why?

"Wait, am I the reason he's not talking to you?"

"Maybe, I don't know. If I knew why he wasn't talking

to me I would fix it."

"Is he really not talking to you or are you just worrying?"

I reassessed our interactions over the last few days.

We'd only really talked about the kids and generic conversations about our days. He hadn't kissed me that morning, but he had still been cuddling me at night. Was there a possibility that I was just imagining it?

"When I think about it, I don't know."

He sent me a shrugging emoji.

I stared, unseeing, at my computer screen. I jumped when my office phone rang.

"Hello?" I said.

"Clare," it was Mum.

"Mum? What's up? Why are you calling my work phone?"

"Hi to you too, I'm having a great day, how about you?"

Proof that your Mum will always try to school you on your manners.

"It's a work day, Mum. What can I do for you?"

"I just wanted to see how you are?"

My fingers tingled in my impatience.

"I'm fine, Mum." I ground out.

"Really? Because I can almost feel the accidental discharge of magic from here."

"Yeah, Mum. Tough day. I'm trying to work out what to do about Michael."

"For now, I'd say calm down. The rest will come to you."

"Thanks." An idea did happen to come to me then. "Hey, can I ask a favour? Can I bring the kids around to your place tonight? Maybe a quiet dinner, just me and Michael will help."

"Sure thing."

"Okay, I'll see you around 4:30?"

"Done. Love you."

"Love you too, Mum."

Now I had a plan. Not one that had me confident

enough for the sweat to stop pouring from my armpits, but a plan nonetheless.

★　　★　　★

I'd read that listening to music can reduce anxiety, so I cranked the tunes while I cooked the dinner.

It had taken a few minutes longer to drop the kids off than I had anticipated, so I recruited a little magical help in my efforts to get the dinner cooked before Michael got home.

I wanted to have the dinner in the oven and the wine glasses full when he arrived.

I sang and danced my way around the kitchen, dodging the knives and spoons that were chopping and mixing as I went.

A spoon brought a taste of bolognaise sauce to my mouth.

"Perfect."

This whisk periodically stirred the pot with the béchamel as it thickened. A block of cheese grated itself next to the baking dish.

I was supervising the knife that was cutting strawberries up to go on top of the pavlova that was almost ready to come out of the oven.

I stacked the meat, béchamel and pasta sheets myself, happy to get my fingers a little dirty on that job.

I had just pulled the pavlova out of the oven and switched it with the lasagne when my phone beeped.

My eyebrows drew together when I saw that it was a text from Michael.

"Just headed out to the pub for a few beers. It was Lucas's last day today."

What? He went to the pub maybe once every six months. *Why tonight?*

I tried to call him.

He rejected the call and texted me.

"I won't be able to hear you in here, sorry."

My chest tightened.

"I've cooked dinner for you."

"Thanks, I'll reheat it when I get home."

What joy I'd found in cooking deflated like a balloon. I could almost hear the fart-like noise moving around the room.

I turned the music off and set a timer for the lasagne.

I figured that if I was going to be eating alone I may as well drink alone too. I poured a generous glass of wine.

Now what do I do?

I briefly thought about going to collect the kids, but couldn't muster up the energy to walk around and then tussle with them. They probably wouldn't want to come home anyway. Mum would be fine.

I thumped a shield over my emotions so Mum didn't become suspicious.

I pottered around the house for a while, picking up the random things littering the floor.

A sock and a pair of knickers under the dining table (I knew better than to wonder how they got there). A doll nappy and stuffed dog in the bathroom. An entire collection of Shopkins and several hair bows in the lounge room.

I did wonder how the hair bows got there. Kaylee and Amaya had begged me to buy about eight of them and then never worn them.

I gave up and sat down with my wine and a book.

My book selections had been narrowed down lately. Murder mysteries made me feel ill – even though I had enjoyed Kathy Reichs novels for years. The tear jerkers just made me anxious about my family – I mean really, Jodi Picoult, the feels. The only thing I'd been able to get lost in was romance.

I skimmed the kindle store and found a new book in the free offerings.

I loved finding new authors that way.

I was three chapters deep and through three quarters of my wine when the timer went off.

I pulled the lasagne out of the oven and left it on the cooktop to cool a little before serving. I realised it was quite late and I hadn't had another message from Michael.

I sent him a text. "What time will you be home?"

"Soon," he said, "Just finishing my beer."

I served a piece of lasagne, covered it in foil and put it in the oven for him. I decided not to wait before he got home to eat, or I would be passed out drunk on the couch.

I refilled my wine and took my dinner back to the armchair in the lounge room. We didn't normally eat in there, because children, but I was home alone and anything goes.

My attention kept wandering from my book as I ate my dinner. I kept checking the time and wondering when I would see Michael.

I jolted awake when the front door opened and Michael tried to stumble in quietly.

He followed the lamplight to find me in the lounge room. I looked to the clock on the mantel.

10:30PM.

"A little late for a school night isn't it?"

"I'm sorry," he said.

"The last message you sent implied you were practically on your way home.

"That was three hours ago."

"Yeah, I know." He grinned sheepishly. "How were the girls?"

"I don't know."

He sobered for a moment. "What do you mean?"

"I sent them to Mum's house so we could have a nice dinner and no frantic rush tonight."

"Oh," he said. "I didn't know."

"You didn't know because you didn't answer your phone when I called you."

"I'm sorry."

He moved in to kiss me and I swayed back at his beer breath.

"Wow, that is fierce. Have you eaten?"

"Not really. Someone ordered some chips, I had a few of those."

"There's some lasagne in the oven for you. I'm going to bed."

He held out a hand to help me stand. My legs were

asleep from being curled under me and I leaned on him for a moment while the fiercest pins and needles passed.

"Thanks," I said, not really wanting to be indebted to him at that particularly moment. "Good night."

"Hey," he grabbed my hand and wheeled me back. "I love you."

I looked up at him, grudgingly, "I love you too."

He pressed a sloppy beer kiss to my lips.

He pulled back and belched. The scent of brewery washed over my face.

"Go have some food." I instructed.

Chapter Twenty Eight

Don't look a gift bottle of wine in the label.

One good thing had come from Michael's night at the pub; it had shaken out whatever bee was under his bonnet and he was speaking to me again.

He came into the bathroom while I was showering to ask if I would like a brewed coffee.

He was in real reconciliation mode, he usually only bothered with the coffee machine on the weekend.

"Are the paw patrol dogs good pups?" I asked.

He opened the shower door to give me a kiss.

He closed the bathroom door behind him and I called out. "Leave that open, please."

"The door?"

"Yeah, I like it open."

"But... It will let all the cold air in."

"It's not that bad."

"You're weird," he said, letting the door swing open.

It did let the cold in, but I didn't like being shut in the bathroom on my own at the moment. There was something a little cold and clinical and isolated about the white tiled echo chamber.

It was also that while I was in the bathroom I didn't really have anything to distract me and it was the prime location for mini-panic attacks and mild freak outs.

My imagination wandered and it didn't usually wander anywhere pleasant.

I wonder what people usually daydream about.

It had been so long since I had day dreamed about

anything other than the disasters that might befall my family that I couldn't really think of anything else.

I decided to muse on possible species of dragon. Should be harmless, right?

Yeah, no.

It only took a few minutes for my mind to roll onto how quickly a dragon could annihilate my family.

Brilliant.

The revitalising aroma of coffee drew me toward the kitchen when I was dressed.

Michael had even packed the lunch boxes for the girls and was boiling eggs. He really was making up for his poor behaviour.

"You do know it's only Friday, don't you? You do have to go to work today."

"I know." He crossed the room to kiss me and pulled me into his arms. "I'm sorry about last night."

"It's not your fault, not completely."

"I've been a bit of a grump this week," he said. "We were trying to finish up a project at work before Lucas left and it was stressful."

He wasn't even grumpy with me after all that worrying!

"You pest, I was worried! I thought you were getting ready to divorce me!"

He laughed, "Why would I do that?"

Suddenly, I felt insecure. I burrowed into his chest and hid my face.

"Clare?" He put his hand on my shoulders and tried to pull me away so he could see my face again.

I muttered a frantic sentence into his shirt, it was unintelligible.

"What?"

I huffed out a breath and looked up at him.

"I thought you were upset and you were going to divorce me because I've been talking to, and seeing, Owen more lately. I thought you might have thought I was having an affair. You would have misunderstood and we would have fought and I would have moved to Mum's house and stayed there at night, but come here early in the morning so the kids wouldn't realise that we'd actually separated until they really had to know."

When I said it out loud it really did sound ridiculous.

Michael apparently agreed. "That's ridiculous!"

"I know, but I couldn't help it."

The hiss of water splashing onto the cooktop interrupted our conversation.

Irritated, I picked up the lid of the pan and set it down next to the cooktop.

"It's just that I've been struggling a bit lately and Doctor Imra thought I might have anxiety. Which it turns out that I do, so I saw a psychologist last week, which is the reason that I started trying to meditate over the weekend."

I felt so much lighter with the confession off my chest, I really should have told him earlier.

But he wasn't even looking at me, not asking questions or offering sympathy.

"Michael, were you even listening to me then?"

He turned back to me, face white. "Did you see that? The lid came off that saucepan on its own!"

Oh, Shopkins!

"It's not exactly that I lied," I said, "I just... didn't tell you."

"You're a witch!" he managed to shout in a whisper.

The word scathed, but I let him have it for now, I'd teach him the importance of the correct nomenclature later.

"Yes, I can do magic."

I had made him sit down at the table after seeing the shock on his face.

I also couldn't believe that I had made such a rookie mistake. Damn.

"Why didn't you ever tell me?"

"It wasn't important." I said.

"How can it not be important?" he asked.

"How is it important?" I countered.

"Well, you could – use magic for the housework, or to get money. Clare, we could quit our jobs and never have to work again!"

"Yeah, it's not quite that simple. Haven't you ever heard of alchemy?"

He stared at me like his brain still hadn't quite kicked back into action.

"Alchemy? Where people tried to turn base metals to gold? The alchemists couldn't do it and neither can the magically abled." I explained. "I think you need a little time to think about this. Why don't you take the day off work and we can talk about it?"

He nodded.

"You eat your breakfast and drink your coffee. I'll go get the girls and take them to school."

A flash of movement drew my eye.

The picture of Mum on the wall winked at me. I scowled.

"When I come back, we can talk."

He nodded.

I passed him his phone and instructed him to call his office, then I rushed out of the house.

He was lying on the couch, looking catatonic, when I returned an hour later.

"You didn't eat your breakfast," he said.

Lack of caffeine; that would explain my headache.

"Thanks, I'll go grab it."

Before I left the room, I surreptitiously picked up any photos with Mum in them and cast a cone of silence.

I zapped the toast, eggs and coffee warm again, then carried it to the armchair to eat.

"What are you, Clare?" he asked.

I pondered how to answer that, there were so many angles to the question.

He sensed my hesitation, "I mean, I know who you are, but I don't know what you are."

"Honey, you've known me for over a third of my life. You've been with me for all the years that formed me.

191

Graduating University, getting our first jobs, buying a house, having kids. You know who I am. *What* I am is no different to that.

"I am a woman, I am your wife, I am the mother of your children, I am a bit of a shitty housewife and I am an anxious mess right now because I've been too busy trying to do everything for everyone that I haven't taken the time to do the things I need to do for myself."

I paused to take a big breath, that sentence had gotten away from me.

"So can we please focus on the relevant issue right now, which is my problem with anxiety rather than you having a little crisis about the fact I can manipulate things with magic."

Michael's faced had paled again and he had squashed himself flat into the couch. His arms were flung over his head and small white beads peppered his clothing.

I'd done it again. Localised Clare-quake with the addition of a little internal gale and some localised hail.

The hail locality was the couch.

"Shit."

I waved my hand and cleared the hail off the couch.

"Sorry, I shouldn't be talking about heavy subjects before I've eaten. Are you hurt?"

"No." He was still laying as stiff as a board on the couch.

"Let's ignore the magic stuff for a minute."

I picked up a piece of toast and chomped on it.

"As long as you stop throwing it at me, it should be fine." His voice was slightly squeaky.

"So, I'm going to assume you didn't hear what I said before on account of the whole saucepan lid being moved around with magic thing.

"I went to the doctor because I've been tired and cranky. Trin made me get my iron levels checked. Doctor Imra made me do these surveys that showed I was at risk for anxiety and she convinced me that was my problem when my iron levels came back normal.

"I saw a psychologist who suggested some techniques

to help with my symptoms, which is why I've been meditating and I have been talking to Owen more because he had panic attacks while we were at Uni."

Michael opted to ask about the most irrelevant part of the story.

"Who's Doctor Imra?"

I groaned, "Really? That's the bit you want to ask about? She's just a Doctor at my work. She's been there for a couple of years; you've met her several times. I can't believe you don't remember.

"Actually, scratch that, I can believe you don't remember. Like you don't remember birthdays, anniversaries and when I ask you to buy milk on the way home from work."

"I just don't understand why I have to get the milk when you work right next to a supermarket." His voice was sullen.

My fingers tingled and my eyes must have flashed with fire as he cowered into the couch again.

"Okay, okay, I'm sorry!

"I think I remember who Doctor Imra is, is she Middle Eastern? I didn't realise she was a lady when you first said, I was trying to picture a guy."

I rolled my eyes.

"Anyway," he said. "What does all this anxiety stuff mean?"

I contemplated my words carefully.

"It means that I've been working too hard... No, that's not quite right. My hormones are out of balance? I think that's a part of it." I growled.

"It basically means that I've got too much stress in my system and I go into these little over the top freak outs like the one I said to you before.

"I overthink scenarios to the point where I have a physical reaction. My heart rate cranks up, I start panting like I've done a lap around the block, I sweat like a pig... It's very unpleasant.

"Or I get stuck in this little worry loop where I just get a tummy ache and want to curl up on the couch and hide from the world."

He forgot his fear of me and crossed the room.

He picked my plate off my lap. He made me stand from my chair. He sat down and he drew me into his lap.

"Oh, Clare," he said, "We've broken you. I'm so sorry."

"It's not your fault," I said.

"Well it isn't your fault," he cupped my face in his hands and kissed me.

I snuggled into his chest and enjoyed the warmth. Being hugged was wonderful, I felt safe and protected.

"When did you find out about the... anxiety?" he asked.

"About three weeks ago." My answer was muffled, I was talking into his shirt in my shame.

Yep, I was ashamed that I hadn't told him. I'd known I should do it all along, I just didn't know how to confess it to him.

His body stiffened and his hands, that had been stroking me, stilled.

"Three weeks? Why are you only telling me this now?"

"I don't know." I pulled my face out so he could hear, and because I was starting to smother. "Because I felt like it would make too much more work for you. Because I was afraid you'd think I wasn't good enough. Because I thought you might decide I wasn't worth the effort and leave me."

He looked hurt, so I jumped in quickly, "I know that isn't what you would have done, but anxiety... it messes with your head.

"Do you really think I would have moved out to my mum's house if our marriage was on the rocks?"

He shook his head.

"That's right, I would have turfed you out on your ear and kept our three-thousand-dollar mattress to myself, thank you very much."

His chest shook and echoed with his laughter.

"It's just that, there's all this other shit combining in my system that leaves me primed for an over the top reaction.

"The kids go on an excursion with school, I worry that one of them will be hit by a bus. You're a little late home from work, I worry that you've had a crash. You don't talk to me for three days and I worry that you're planning to leave me anyway.

"And sometimes those little worry sessions just distract me from my work, but sometimes they blow out to a full panic attack."

He nodded and I let him absorb all the information.

I reached for my untouched coffee and cradled it in my hands. It was cold again.

I harnessed some magic in the air, warmed up my fingers and let it pass into the coffee cup until the liquid steamed again.

Michael watched me, gaze sharpening when the smell of warm coffee filled his nose.

"Did you just heat that up with magic?"

I nodded, blushing a little.

"Why don't you ever do that with your feet at night instead of trying to cryogenically freeze mine off?"

I laughed.

"It's not as easy as all that. Have we finished with the anxiety for a minute, do you want to talk about the magic?"

"Yeah," he said, "And for the record I expect you to never serve me a cold steak again!"

I stiffened and he defended his statement.

"Kidding, I'm kidding. Geez, no need to singe my eyebrows off."

I subsided.

"So, how long have you been a witch?" he asked, "Is it a from birth thing? Were you cursed by an evil wizard? Dunked in toxic waste as part of a secret Government program?"

I rolled my eyes and whacked his chest, "Can you ever be serious for more than one minute as a time?"

"Honey, I'm as serious as that shit storm you hailed down on me earlier."

I snorted.

"Why do you think I came over here? Now you're shielding me from any more localised hail events."

I glared at him, "You are so annoying."

"I know, it's amazing I've lasted this long when I think about it now. Tell me about magic, witchy woman."

I schooled him in the importance of a non-gender specific term in the world of magical manipulation.

"So, does that mean I can get out of doing housework ever again? Because you can just wave your fingers and poof! The dirt is gone."

I laughed, "Unfortunately for you, no."

He gave me a pantomime frown.

"It's not that simple." I said, "Yes, I could use magic to do everything, but the time I would have to spend preparing crystals would make the time saved on housework pointless."

We had shifted to the long sofa so we could see each other's faces, but still maintained contact along the length of our bodies.

"So, the crystals store your power?"

"No. The basic explanation is that it saves us from experiencing magical whiplash. It's like balancing out the recoil on a gun, so you don't break your shoulder when you fire a rifle."

"What's the whiplash like without it?"

"Remember the other week when I was stuck in bed for the whole day and Mum took the kids?"

"Oh." Understanding crossed his face, then an expression like mine when waiting for his water cooler gossip. "So what magic had you done?"

I told him about the incident with the kid in the car park.

"Wow," he looked at me like I really was Super Mum, "You saved that kid's life."

I shrugged and wriggled under his gaze, "I did what any other person would have done."

"Not quite, I wouldn't have been able to stop time."

"Well," I said, a blush rising, "You would have done

something."

He picked up one of my hands and kissed my palm. Puzzlement crossed his face.

"Have you ever had to do magic to save our kids?"

My stomach clenched. I had been waiting for this question.

"I don't want to tell you." I hid my face with my hands.

He moved so his body was over mine, the warm weight of him squishing me into the couch.

"Clare?"

His breath fell on my hands. His hands held my wrists. He didn't try to pull my hands away, just waited.

I moved my fingers to make gaps to peek at him through.

"No, it's too terrible."

"Clare," his tone was even, but it held a hidden edge, "You're scaring me."

I couldn't tell if the pressure in my chest was from panic or his weight on me.

"Fine. Isetfiretothekitchen."

"Could you say that slower?"

I removed my hands and made him sit up. It was getting hard to breathe.

I caught his attention and told him the story that still made me break out in a cold sweat, even years later.

When I finished, my conscience felt the lack of it. One less coal lump of guilt to keep hidden inside.

Michael's face was bone-white.

He pulled me into a hug and squeezed.

"I'm so glad it was you and not me," he said.

"Oh gee, thanks!"

"That came out wrong. I mean, I would have been completely powerless in that situation, I'm so glad it was you, who could fix it. You saved our children and our home."

I reserved acceptance of his worship. "It wouldn't have happened at all if I hadn't left the pan on while I left the room."

He kissed me fiercely, "Honey, accidents happen all the time, it wasn't your fault."

Those words released a piece of shame I hadn't even realised I was harbouring.

Unbidden, tears streamed from my eyes and I sobbed on him again.

He rubbed my back while I cried, releasing all the pent-up emotions I had from that event; guilt, shame and fear.

I hadn't even told Mum about that.

Naturally, she knew something big had happened. She'd told me she would have felt that magical expenditure from Tasmania. She had nursed me through the backlash and looked after the kids for me.

And I'd been the ungrateful shit that hadn't even told her what happened.

Although, she'd never pressed for the story, she had probably scried it out.

★　　★　　★

"What I want to know," Michael said.

He stopped talking to concentrate on the sandwiches he was making for our lunch. He was very good at having the first half of a conversation in his head and then bringing me in halfway without actually telling me what we were talking about. Also at picking up a conversation several hours after we'd started it.

"What do you want to know?"

He was completely focussed on aligning the cheese just right on our sandwiches. He was very fussy with his sandwiches.

"What?" I asked again.

"Could you pass the mayonnaise, please?"

I slammed the offending condiment down on the bench.

"What?!"

He put the top bread on the sandwiches and looked at me. He didn't waver under my glower.

"Does that mean our children are suddenly going to learn they can make things dance around the room like in

Matilda?"

I rolled my eyes at him, "I hope not. The headaches they'd get after that would be enough to turn them off it for life.

"Mum and I will keep an eye on them, see if they start showing any signs of magic."

His face brightened, "I just realised something."

That look always worried me. "What?"

"My mother-in- law really is a witch!"

I threw a tea towel at his face.

Chapter Twenty Nine

Motherhood – Where your children get a new t-shirt every two weeks and you are wearing the same daggy knickers you had before they were born.

Friday's confessions left me emotionally – and therefore physically – drained.

Saturday morning came about and I felt like a half set jelly.

I decided to try a new relaxation technique. Mum had given me a host of herbal remedy suggestions; I opted to try peppermint tea.

I also decided to shelve the baby blanket I was crocheting for a little while and try something fun.

My tea was brewing and I was looking through my yarn stash in the corner of the lounge room when Kaylee came running in from the backyard.

"Mum! Dad! Come and see this, Amaya has got some of her birds and it's so cool!!"

I looked up at Michael, sitting in an armchair with his tablet and a coffee. He raised his eyebrows at me.

I shrugged and stood.

"We'd best see this together," I said.

When we walked through the kitchen I spotted Razzle hiding under the dining table.

"They're bigger than me," the kitten said in a small voice.

Apprehension gnawed at my stomach.

It took a moment to spot Amaya when we stepped out onto the deck. Her giggle drew my attention to a patch of lawn, next to the agapanthus, in the shade of the gum tree.

She was sitting with her legs outstretched, a juvenile galah sat on her left shoulder

And a juvenile galah perched on her right arm.

And a juvenile galah perched on her left leg.

And a juvenile galah sat next to her right leg, chewing on the hem of her skirt.

It was a hokey-pokey of galahs.

Amaya giggled again, "Your claws are tickling me."

A loud squawk from the roof of the cubby caught my attention. Dash was chuckling away on the roof peak.

"I guess your hatchlings have started fledging then?" I asked.

The galah was too busy laughing to answer me.

"Errr, honey?" Michael's voice sounded weak, "Is this the sort of sign you look out for? For whether the kids are magic?"

I couldn't help myself, I laughed.

"I'm not sure I see the humour here." Michael said.

Kaylee had crossed the yard and was scratching the neck of one of the babies.

I held my hand up and concentrated for a moment, listening to the chatter of the babies to see if any were in conversation with the either of the kids.

I turned to Michael.

"It's fine. The girls aren't talking to the birds. They are just the babies of some birds I've known since I was a teenager."

He swallowed hard. "Right."

I smiled, "It's okay. The kids are safe. The bird father is on the cubby."

I turned to point to Dash but found the roof of the cubby empty.

I heard a whoosh of feathers and Michael's sharp intake of breath.

"Uh, honey?"

I covered my smile.

Dash sat on Michael's shoulder, preening his feathers and looking proud of himself.

"Michael, meet Dash. Dash, be nice to my husband."

Dash dropped his wing to his body and tried to look innocent.

"Dash? Please don't bite my ear off."

Dash responded with a gentle nip on his earlobe. Michael stiffened.

"Tell him I won't bite hard."

I relayed Dash's message.

A flurry of squawks came from the sky over the fence.

It was Eneya. She didn't sound pleased.

She descended on Dash like a fury.

Michael saw eight outstretched talons coming toward him and bolted into the house. He seemed to have forgotten about the bird still perched on his shoulder.

Eneya gripped the screen door and screeched.

"Dash?! Dash?! Rat of the winds! Hide in the human nest you cannot!"

I put my fingers on the line and reached a hand out to the furious mother bird.

"Eneya? Eneya!"

"Clare!" She shrieked, unable to drop her anger to talk to me. "That bird! I went hunt. Return to nest! No hatchlings! No Dash! Pluck his flight feathers and leave him to predators!"

Her speech had reverted to basic bird.

"Ah, the hatchlings weren't meant to be ready to fly yet?"

"No!" She screeched, then seemed to realise that she was talking to me instead of Dash, "I expected more sunrises. I suspect he taught without me. Then fly here to prank you! And angry me!"

She finally stepped off the door and let me smooth her ruffled feathers.

I spied movement in the corner of my eye and saw Michael standing at the window.

"Dash?" I mouthed to him.

He pointed to the bench next to the window.

I mimed opening the window.

His eyes widened and he shook his head.

"Trust me," I mimed.

He threw his eyes skyward, and opened the window.

Dash showed how he earned his name and took off as soon as the gap was big enough to escape through.

Eneya's fury was reignited and she took to the air, chasing her life partner and squawking parrot obscenities at him.

"What about them?"

Michael pointed at Kaylee, Amaya and the four juvenile galahs.

I smiled and shrugged, "There's a jar of sunflower seeds under the sink. Dash and Eneya will come back in a little while."

I crossed the lawn to sit with the girls and the birds.

Michael joined us, the jar of sunflower seeds in hand.

We sat in the shade for a long while, feeding the birds and enjoying the fresh air.

This was the kind of crazy I could handle in my life.

"Clare?"

Michael interrupted my late night Sudoku. The click of his phone locking and the thud of it on the bedside table indicated he was ready for sleep.

"Yeah?"

"I was just wondering... have you ever used magic, to, you know..."

He stumbled over his words. I put my own phone down and rolled over to look at him.

"What?"

"Love potions?"

I smiled, "Are you worried I used magic to make you fall in love with me?"

His smile was a little sheepish, "Yeah, I guess."

I kissed him, "Yes, it's possible to make love potions, but I've never used one. Although, if I'd had a chance to meet Justin Timberlake when I was a teenager my life might be completely different."

He chuckled quietly.

"The way I see it," I said, "Love has a magic all of its

own. If I have to manipulate someone into loving me, what's the point?"

He smiled and pressed a gentle kiss to my lips.

I was struck by a sudden idea.

"Can I show you something?"

He shrugged, "Sure."

I rested my head on his chest and made the ceiling my canvas.

I painted pictures of light for him, drawing inspiration from my memories.

I drew our family. Smiles, knotty hair, dirty faces in all their glory.

I allowed each picture to hold for a few minutes, studying the features and faces of our babies. Then I dissolved them and let the colours boil and resolve into new pictures; new images of our beautiful, chaotic lives.

He pressed a kiss to my head when I finally let the colours dissolve and the room fell into darkness.

He cleared his throat.

"Those were beautiful."

I noticed tears in the corners of his eyes.

I rolled over and up and kissed him properly.

"Plus," he smiled, "Now I can tell my friends that my wife is really magical in the bedroom."

I barked a short laugh and whacked him in the face with my pillow.

We kissed again and progressed to making magic together.

Chapter Thirty

More than just the power bill can change in three months.

"Mummy!" came the scream.

"Aaargh, Mama," The wailing gradually drew nearer.

I sighed.

I would never get to watch this episode of Grand Designs.

I jumped from my seat and met them at the kitchen door. Amaya had an arm over Kaylee's shoulder and the eldest answered my unspoken question.

"Amaya rolled her ankle on the trampoline."

"Oh dear. Can you please help her to the lounge room? I'll grab an ice pack."

Kaylee was sliding a pillow under Amaya's ankle on the couch when I got in there.

Moments like that warmed my heart in the middle of the screaming fits. Well, maybe not in the middle of the screaming fits, but they certainly lingered in my mind longer than the arguments.

Don't get me wrong, three months in the lives of my children had not suddenly turned them into perfectly behaved model children, but my reactions to their bad didn't seem to be as fierce.

"Do you two want to watch this show with me? It's got bulldozers and cranes and all sorts of cool things."

"Yeah," Kaylee said.

Amaya just pleaded, "Mama."

I instructed her to shuffle up so I could sit. She laid her head down in my lap and I pressed 'play' on the video.

A minute later, Kaylee whined, "There's too much talking in this show."

She dragged 'talking' out to a full three seconds.

I paused the show.

"Alright," I said, "I'll do you a deal, let me watch one episode of this and I'll let you choose a movie on Netflix after. I'll even make popcorn for you."

"Oooh!" said Kaylee.

Amaya, detail oriented, said, "Who gets to choose the movie?"

"You can, because you hurt your ankle."

"That's not fai-"

Kaylee stopped talking when I held up a finger.

"Fine," she begrudged.

"Excellent." I pressed play again.

We settled back, I played with Amaya's hair as she rested on my lap.

I reached for my cup of tea and realised it was on the little table at the other end of the couch.

I made sure the kids were both paying attention the TV and levitated it behind the couch and into my hand.

Razzle snorted from the armchair.

"Hush, you," I said to him, "Or I'll start buying the cheap cat food."

Michael had been right. The cat had been good for me.

There had been many times when he'd sensed me spiralling from worry to panic and jumped into my lap. His kneading had sometimes been a little brutal, I'd threatened to declaw him a few times, but on the whole, he had helped reduce my stress levels.

The flip-flip of the cat flap in kitchen sounded. I raised my eyebrow at Razzle.

"A friend of yours?"

"Not my friend."

Tapping claws sounded on the floorboards in the passage.

The sound stopped at the door to the lounge room.

When I strained my ears, I made out the quiet

padding of little feet on the carpet. A whoosh of air and the galah landed on the couch next to my head.

Eight little claws spiked into my scalp near my forehead.

A little pink and white head peered down to look in my eyes.

"Hi, Dash."

Dash groomed my hair in greeting. I reached up to scratch his little head.

A quiet meow drew my attention to the armchair.

Dash gave a low squawk. Razzle rose and slowly approached the lounge.

The cat still had a lean little body and he hadn't quite grown into his paws.

Razzle jumped onto the arm of the sofa and climbed up to sniff at Dash's face. Dash gently twiddled a whisker in his beak. Razzle butted his head against Dash's wing.

It had taken several weeks, but, despite his objections, Razzle had made friends with the two birds.

On several occasions, I had found the three snoozing in the sunlight. Razzle's black and white body in sphinx pose, Dash and Eneya perched contentedly on his back.

Seeing them together always helped drain a little tension from my body.

★ ★ ★

"Hey, Clare, head in. Would you like a cup of tea or some cold water?"

Rachel's greeting had become as familiar as her office over the last few months.

"No, thanks." I smiled, "I'm good."

I settled into the patient seat and waited for her.

I noticed that my waiting habits had changed.

In the past I would have pulled out my phone to fill in the few minutes of wait time. Or mentally log the jobs that were waiting for my return home that night. It would have been the perfect opportunity to worry about my children or my husband and spiral into an anxious moment.

Now, I was happy to sit and wait. I studied the artwork on the wall; it looked like one of the classic artists.

A child on a beach at sunset.

"How have you been, Clare?"

The door clicked closed behind her.

I shot her a sunny smile.

"Pretty good, actually. I haven't shouted at my kids at all this week."

Never mind that it was only Tuesday.

"Wow!" Rachel smiled, "That's really good, I know that was one of the things you really didn't like.

"And how are you going with those anxious thoughts?"

I thought before answering, "Better, I think. I'm getting much better at recognising them when they appear. I can accept them and dismiss them before it turns into a worry session."

"Well done. I'm really proud of you."

I smiled and blushed slightly. No matter who it was, it was always good to have someone say those words to you.

"And how are you going with your artwork?"

Now there was a drastic change. Michael had planted a seed that had really taken root.

Of course, Rachel didn't know the full details on my chosen medium – Magic mixed with oil on canvas.

My paintings were best described as abstract. A seemingly random mix of colours splashed across a canvas. But people said they were joyful and I was starting to sell them.

I wasn't making money from them, but I was covering the cost of the materials, which was nice. Etsy for the win!

I told her about my most recent commission piece – a 1.5m x 2m panoramic piece for a friend's new house.

It was exciting to work closely with someone to give them something beautiful and it would make me so happy to see it hanging on the wall when the house was built.

"Excellent!"

We shared broad smiles.

"Well," she said, "I think that's all we need to do for today, why don't you make another appointment to see me in a couple of months to touch base?"

"Sounds great, thank you."

I shook the psychologist's hand and left the office.

Dinner that night was a raucous affair.

Trin, Frank, Sian and Arlo joined us for dinner.

In the interest of my sanity, I had made the decision to reduce my alcohol intake in recent months, so I declined the pre-dinner wine.

Trin made a little moue at me, but settled for the mock-mojito starter.

"I can't believe it's not alcohol!" She winked at me when she took her first sip.

I rolled my eyes at her.

"You know there's no peer pressure here, you can get rolling drunk if you want to. I'll just come round and laugh at you when you have a hangover in the morning." I said.

"You are so evil."

The evening was full of laughter, crazy children antics and a little bit of magic (when I accidentally burned the lasagne).

By the time the guests left, the children were completely wound up and wild with overtiredness.

It took a long bath, a short teeth brush and three stories to finally get the kids calm enough to lay down for sleep.

Michael left me to give Amaya one extra cuddle so he could get started on the dishes.

"No Mama, I want you to stay with me."

Her arms could still grip like a vice.

"I know baby, I know."

My heart rate started to rise, I needed my quiet time tonight too! My fingers tingled.

Calm down you, I said to my misbehaving digits.

I squeezed her tight.

"Oh, my little hot water bottle."

She giggled.

Kaylee grumbled, we were keeping her awake.

"Alright, darling, I'm going to go now. I love you and I'll see you in the morning."

I pulled my head down and out of her grasp.

"Ah, ah, ah," she said.

"What's wrong?"

"I need my unicorns."

"Which ones? And where are they?"

She listed three stuffed unicorns and their locations. She was remarkably good at remembering where they were, but not to take them to bed.

I planted last bedtime kisses and gave each a last bedtime cuddle and tried to make my escape.

I made it to the door.

"Mama," Amaya's said in a voice that could make Chantilly cream taste as salty as pickled pork.

Oh sweet lord, what now?

"Yes darling?"

"I love you."

My heart melted, exploded, glowed and expanded to the size of the city.

"I love you too, sweetheart."

Michael joined me on the couch when he finished setting the kitchen to rights.

I was exhausted and should have gone straight to bed, but I wanted the time to relax and catch up on my Sudoku.

Plus, I was overdue for one of Michael's award-winning foot rubs.

Yes, I said award-winning. He had won the trophy for 'most likely man to rub my feet in a manner that made me melt'.

It was a narrow field, but he most definitely topped it.

"Is it an air art night tonight?"

"I don't know if I'll even be able to raise a pinkie after that foot rub. You dissolved my brain, and magical abilities along with it."

"I'd better stop then. I need you to function, without you we'd turn into wild creatures, roaming the neighbourhood for edible herbs."

"Just don't eat the ones with the seven-pointed leaves with serrated edges. I'm pretty sure I've seen some of those in the back garden a few doors down."

He laughed, "I'll keep that in mind."

"Come on," I said, "Let's go to bed."

He stood and hauled me to my feet.

We kissed and he dragged me to the bedroom.

My phone dinged from my back pocket.

Michael's head drooped and I laughed.

"Saved by the bell," I laughed.

I opened the screen, clicked the link and laughed again.

Michael narrowed his eyes.

"Owen again?"

I nodded through my laughter.

Michael beckoned to the phone.

It was security camera footage of a kid dancing out on a front veranda while no-one was looking.

"I could totally imagine Amaya doing that." I said.

A huge yawn split my face.

Michael offered me a gentle smile, "Come on Magic Mama, to bed with you."

We snuggled up together and I didn't need my Sudoku to fall gently to sleep.

Afterword

Dear Reader,

This book hatched because I wanted to write a story about my daily laughs and struggles with parenthood, the mother load, my day job and myself. I wanted to write something about taking humour where you can get it (even if it's from perfectly timed flatulence) and trying your best to make it through each day.

The problem was that I couldn't see how to structure a beginning, middle and end for a parenting story. From everything I've heard, you never really stop worrying about your children and the stresses seem to morph rather than disappear.

After mulling the problem over for several months, I finally remembered what a wonderful fellow author once told me – write what you know. From there, the idea to roll some of my struggles with Generalised Anxiety Disorder grew.

In any year, approximately 1 in 5 Australians will experience a mental health disorder. That's an astonishingly large number.

So, think about the people who surround you, how many people are in your life – family, friends, work colleagues. How many people are you friends with on Facebook?

And how many of them have mentioned a mental health condition this year?

Now compare the 1 in 5 chance of a mental health disorder with the roughly 1 in 20 chance of being diagnosed with a new case of cancer (an estimated 138,321 new cases of cancer will be diagnosed in 2018) and think about the coverage and exposure each condition is given...

So you have a four times greater chance of experiencing a mental health condition this year than being diagnosed with a new cancer.

Yet the stigma against mental health is still so strong, men are shamed for their emotions and suicide is the leading cause of death for Australians between 15 and 44 years of age.

It's a confronting statistic, and can be a lethal condition.

Once I had the idea of including an anxiety disorder in this book, it became a way to reduce the stigma. Representing mental health issues in a normal light (not a positive light, or a negative light, but just as a normal, fact of life light) is important and maybe it will help you or one of the twenty per cent of the people you know put their hand up and say they have struggled too.

We're only here for a short time and there's no room for feeling bad about your feelings, shutting yourself away because you don't feel good enough, clothes with inadequate pockets or bad chocolate.

Katie xo

Acknowledgements

Thank you to all the readers who have been with me and encourage me on my journey as a writer. Seeing that someone has faith in you and trusts your ability as a writer is always a wonderful thing. Every time I pitch a book to someone and make a sale, I get a little thrill, it's awesome.

Thank you to my extended family who help out my little family so I can travel the country and share my words with others.

For this book, I owe a lot to my family.

A lot of the little family anecdotes in this book come from my family life. You honestly couldn't make up some of the stuff that comes of my kids mouths sometimes.

So thank you to my kids, for being the crazy, loving, beasts that you are.

And, as always, thank you to my husband, for accepting me whether I'm affectionate, anxious, hangry or deep in a creative kick and don't emerge for days. I love you.